The Hurricane Party

Also by Chuck Morgue

The Horns Of Evangelina
The Main Course

THE HURRICANE PARTY

CHUCK MORGUE

HOUSE OF MORGUE

2010

THE HURRICANE PARTY

Copyright © 2010 Chuck Morgue

Cover art and design by Chuck Morgue
Author photos by Fallon Marie Morgue

Published by House Of Morgue

For contact information visit:
www.houseofmorgue.com

ISBN 978-0-615-35441-5

FIRST EDITION

10 9 8 7 6 5 4 3 2 1

A NOTE FROM THE AUTHOR

The Hurricane Party is a literal work of exploitation fiction. The levels of vicious immorality this book descends to will certainly leave most readers disgusted, offended and ashamed for having delved into it's dark pages. This book is filled with unbridled perversities and inhuman atrocities. This book is a sin against all that is pure and righteous. There is no redemption for those who read this tale of absolute madness.

If you venture any further than this you will be caught in a perfect storm of sadistic sickness, and there is no high ground for you to seek refuge upon.

Foolish reader, you have been warned.

To dedicate this book to anyone would be incomprehensible. There is no one on Earth whom I loathe enough to consecrate this awful tale to.

Instead, I shall offer my sympathies to certain individuals.

Mister Craven. Mister Hooper. Mister Deodato. Mister Roth. Mister Riggs. Mister Harris. Mister Frith. Mister Bonin. Mister Hannagriff. Mister Johnson. Mistress Gayle. Mister Zombie. Mister Aja. Mistress Brite.   Mister Barker. Mister Poe. Mister Laugier. Mister Bataille. Mister Baudelaire. Doctor Suglia. Mistress Fallon. Young Isabelle. Young Rowan. Young Alexander. Young Helena. My dear Mother, Father, Sister and Brother, whom I pray shall never set eyes upon this ghastly work.

And most importantly, Mister Morgue. It is to myself I owe the greatest apology. The thought that such a story as this could spill from your mind, I am afraid you may have finally, ultimately passed on to a darker side of existence. May god's mercy be with you, for there is no longer any hope for your mortal soul.

In memory of Ron Asheton and Lux Interior, because The Stooges and The Cramps were the real rock and roll shit.

THE HURRICANE PARTY

Personally, I think that the unique and supreme delight lies in the certainty of doing 'evil' -- and men and women know from birth that all pleasure lies in evil.

Charles Baudelaire

The old house in the woods of DeQuincy, just northwest of the city of Lake Charles, Louisiana, cannot seem to get properly cleaned. Wearing his father's black bathrobe, with his mother's yellow rubber gloves, John has been mopping and scrubbing and wiping for hours. The progress seems slow. Protracted. Almost futile.

On the radio, "Keep Yourself Alive" by the seventies rock icons Queen is booming out from local station KMRG 99.9 FM.

The large house was a real fixer-upper when his parents bought it about two years ago. His father was going to do most of the work himself, with John helping when possible. When his parents were killed in a car accident a little over a year ago, John inherited the house. As well as the work that would go into it.

John was reluctant at first, but he quickly began to enjoy working on the place. His father's insurance policy left him a surprising amount of money, and he has funneled a good bit of it into the house.

John has made it his mission to make this house his home. To make it his own. It is all he has left.

In the last couple of weeks he has pretty much finished the main work on the house, and has been dying to show it off. Although now he is beginning to wonder if inviting his friends for the weekend was not a mistake. The place is such a mess. He just can't seem to get it clean.

So much mess. This had to be a mistake.

John steps out on the small front porch and looks up to the sky. A cool breeze blows through his shaggy, dirty blonde hair. He sees only a few dark clouds. But he knows, this time of year, the rain is never far.

The rain is never far.

Hey everybody this is Coolhand Madman and I'm gonna be keeping you company all weekend long. I have diligently volunteered to be your eyes and ears during the hurricane this weekend, for all you guys and girls who decided to throw the bird at the Governor and ignore the evacuation order. We know a lot of you either have no way to leave or nowhere to go, and some of you just don't think things are going to get that bad. Well, I just want to let you know that things are definitely going to get bad. Really friggin' bad. You thought Hurricanes Katrina and Rita were monsters, well Hurricane Bataille is one bad mother- SHUT MY MOUTH! Already a Category 5 storm, the experts are predicting Hurricane Bataille will be Cat 6 before making landfall tomorrow night around 9:00 PM. So get those windows boarded, get your pets inside, and make sure your generators are topped off with gas. And be sure to keep your radios tuned to this station, KMRG 99.9, southwest Louisiana's number one source for news and the best classic and modern rock. We're gonna kick off this weekend hurricane party with AC/DC. This is "Thunderstruck," on KMRG, the Mighty Rock Gods, 99.9 FM. The time is 7:30 AM.

"Son of a fuckin' bitch!"

Elise grips the edge of her seat as the van
makes a hard right turn on the unmarked gravel
road. Her boyfriend Gary just laughs his ass off
from the driver's seat beside her. He is wearing
green cargo shorts and Adidas shoes, with an LSU
Tigers t-shirt. His long brown hair is pulled back
into a ponytail. Some of the hairs are not long
enough to be held by the ponytail, so a few strands
hang down in his face, tickling his cheeks. Elise is
wearing blue jeans and a purple ¾ sleeved v-neck t-
shirt. She is wearing purple sandals. Her long
auburn hair is in a loose ponytail.

"How much further?" Elise asks.

"About two miles," Gary says. "It's the only
house back here. This road is pretty much a long-ass
private driveway."

This is not totally true. Along the side of the
road, surrounded by woods and a few scattered
clearings, the van passes a couple of small camper
trailers, covered in overgrown weeds and vines.

Whether or not anyone lives in them, who could say? They look abandoned, but the Cajun trash down here keep their homes in a perpetual state of decay anyway.

"I forgot how fucking creepy it is back here," Maggie says from one of the middle seats. Maggie's light-toned black skin gets goose bumps with every bump the van hits. She nervously reaches up and pushes hair out of her face, tucking it behind her ear. Her hair, naturally black and curly, has light blue highlights, which was a bitch to get just right. Most black girls would simply get colored extensions, or that shitty temporary hair paint, but Maggie always wants the real thing. She is wearing a burgundy tank top, her favorite for nearly ten years, worn out to perfection, and a long black flowing skirt with burgundy-tinted leather fuck-me boots. Around her neck is a necklace with a silver pendant. Two fish. Her zodiac sign. Pisces. She feels that she is looking rather spectacular, and is hoping that Wesley has taken notice.

"The house should look nice," Wesley says, his arm around Maggie. John is a typical prep, but he used to be one of the slacker rock and rollers in high school. His short black hair, in delicate spikes, used to be long and flowing. His left eyebrow piercing healed over a year ago. And he long ago traded his fishnet shirts and leather jacket for what he is wearing today. Kaki pants and a navy blue collared dress shirt. He still wears heavy black Doc Martin boots, the only connection he displays to his former rebellious self. "John said he's done a ton of work on the place. I can't wait to see it."

"Be good to see him too," Gary adds.

"Would you please get your suitcase off my bags," Frankie moans from the backseat.

Taylor, Gary's younger sister, pulls the headphones of her iPod out of her ears, the high-pitched and distorted tones of Marilyn Manson's "I Want To Kill You Like They Did In The Movies" becoming slightly audible to the rest of the van. She is wearing black jeans, and a black tank top with a Misfits logo screen printed on front. She is wearing neon green Converse high tops, and pink and black stripped socks and arm bands. Her long blonde hair is braided into pigtails, with the color red dyed into the tips. She glares at Frankie, sitting nearby.

"What?"

"Your suitcase," Frankie repeats to her. "It's on my bags."

"So?"

"So?! I have valuable items in my bags," Frankie whines.

"Like what?" Taylor asks, disinterested.

"You're messing up his comic books!" Gary calls out from the front.

"Comic books?" Taylor asks Frankie.

"They are very important to me," Frankie says.

Taylor stares at him for a moment. "Like I give a shit about your fucking comic books. It's bad enough I had to sit back here with you."

"Do you have to be such a pretentious bitch?"

"Hey!" Gary yells. "Why don't you two quit arguing. Or get married already or something."

"Uh, no thanks," Taylor says. "I don't marry fags."

She reaches down and moves her suitcase off of Frankie's bags. She glares at him again, briefly, before putting her headphones back in place, retreating back into her gothic solitude.

Frankie readjusts his bags, and stares out the window at the vast nature spread out around them. He is your stereotypical nerd. Wearing a brown cardigan sweater over a Captain America t-shirt, with horn-rimmed glasses and short black hair, with a small cowlick in the back of his head which has been there as long as he can remember.

"Are there bears out here?" Frankie asks.

"No," Wesley answers. "The snakes are pretty bad, though. And alligators."

"Think we'll see one?"

"Dude, I'll help you catch one and eat it," Gary says, turning left into another sharp curve.

"I think I'll pass," Frankie says, pushing his glasses back up the bridge of his nose.

Coming out of the curve, the road widens into a clearing and just ahead they see their destination, John's house.

"This is gonna be fucking awesome," Gary says, smiling as he sees John sitting on the front porch steps of the house.

John stands up with a nervous wave as the van comes to a stop, horn blowing brashly. He is wearing blue jeans, a red and black flannel shirt, and a black t-shirt with a picture of country music legend Johnny Cash on the front. In the picture, Johnny Cash is making a goofy face while flipping the bird at whoever was taking the original photograph.

"Hey cocksucker!" Gary shouts, throwing open the driver's door.

"Gary," John says, smiling. "How was the trip?"

"Long as fuck, dude."

Gary walks up to John and they embrace in a long overdue hug. The others begin to pour out of the van, and John's eyes widen a little when he sees

Maggie.

"Hey bro," Wesley says, grabbing Maggie's hand, pulling her along behind him. "I can't believe we finally made it."

"I'm glad you did," John says, hugging his friend. He then nervously looks at Maggie. "Hey."

"Hey," she says. After an awkward moment, she reaches out her arms and hugs John. "The house looks amazing. I can't believe you did all this."

"Thanks," John says. "Wait till you see the inside."

"Dude," Gary says. "I want you to meet my sweetie. This is Elise."

Elise extends her hand. John takes it, exchanging hellos.

"And this is Frankie," Gary says, motioning to the skinny nerd with the glasses.

"Gary's roommate," John says, extending his hand for Frankie. Frankie just stands there, staring at John's hand.

"I don't shake," Frankie says. "Nothing personal."

"Okay…" John says.

"Don't mind him," Gary butts in. "Frankie's

kind of weird and shit, but he's good people. Smartest motherfucker I know."

John is then distracted by the sight of Taylor walking up carrying her suitcase and backpack.

"Gary," John says. "Why is your sister here?"

"I know," Gary says. "I didn't ask. I didn't think you'd mind. Our parents are going through their bullshit again, and I figured it would be good for her to get away from all that for a few days."

"I wish you had said something," John says.

"I'm sorry, man," Gary says. "Is it cool?"

"I guess so."

John looks around at everybody, taking in the sight of all his friends together. It's been so long since he's seen them. "Well then," he says. "Let's get inside. I'm sure you all want to stretch out a little."

They all head up into the house. John looks out around the yard. He takes his cell phone from his pocket, quickly scrolls through menus, hitting buttons before following his friends and shutting the door.

"Just checked the weather," he says. "Storm's supposed to hit tomorrow night. We've got about thirty-six hours until all hell breaks loose."

"Well," Gary says. "We'd better get this mother fucker started then."

Okay, let's go to Matt Bonin, our guy in the sky, for a quick weather update--

"Thanks, Cool. I am flying over the coast right now, a little east of Cameron, and I am looking out at the Gulf Of Mexico. I can see black sky stretching out for hundreds of miles. Somewhere out in that heavy void, Hurricane Bataille is churning away like the Tazmanian Devil in one of those old Warners' cartoons. The wind is getting pretty rough, and I'm pretty sure this will be the last trip I make into the air to cover this storm. It's, um, safe to say we may be looking at some rain tomorrow morning. By the afternoon at the latest."

Matt, can you tell us about the people in the community there? Earlier today the Governor declared a mandatory evacuation for the majority of southwest Louisiana.

"Yes, Cool, and I believe the Governor of Texas made a similar announcement earlier as well, for his citizens from Houston and Beaumont and elsewhere. From what I have seen, most of the people down here have left for higher ground *already. This is a Category 5 storm and obviously it is in everyone's best interest to get out of the way. I should note that as usual quite a few people have made the decision to ride out the storm, for whatever reason, but if at all possible I hope they will get in their cars and head north. It is just foolish to sit and wait for this monster to come knocking on their doors. If they are home to answer the door, they're gonna find themselves in a world of trouble. There are only about eighteen hours left until the storm makes landfall, so I hope people move fast."*

And Matt, what do you plan to do for those next eighteen hours?

"Well, Cool, I'm going home, boarding up my windows, and getting out of dodge. I think you are more than capable and crazy enough to run this show on your own! (laughs)"

And that was our airborne weather reporter Matt Bonin updating us on the approach of Hurricane Bataille down on the Gulf coast. Now it's time to get back to the rock. How's about a little Ratt, "Round And Round," since that's what the hurricane is doing out there, going round and round. I know, that's a bit of a stretch, but I want some 80s metal, and finding storm references is turning out to be a little tougher than I first thought. Gimme a break, mofos. You're listening to KMRG 99.9 FM.

John watches his friends. It feels bittersweet to see them all, sitting around his living room. Drinking. Laughing. Talking about old times. John has been through so much pain over the last year or so, has been on depression medicine, has been working himself to death trying to get this house up to par. But deep down, he is comforted by their presence. His parents are dead. This is practically the only family he has left. He stares at Maggie.

He looks around at the shelves and cabinets and drawers that take up so much space. Filled with photographs, CDs, DVDs, cassettes, books, all sorts of things. He has a label-maker in the kitchen, and has used it to make labels for almost everything in the house. He has become a little obsessive with it, and he notices that there is a little black label marked TELEVISION stuck to the side of the TV set. There are labels marked REFRIGERATOR, FRONT DOOR, TV REMOTE, MICROWAVE, PAPERBACKS, RECORDS, BILLS, CLOSET, MIRROR, BED, WINDOW, DESK, TABLE, MAC (on his laptop in the bedroom), anything and everything has a label, no matter how redundant the label might be. This is the first time he has noticed the odd extent of his labeling. Perhaps he has been spending too much time in the house. He just hopes no one brings it up. He's feeling a little embarrassed just thinking about it.

"So, John, what's your favorite song?" Elise asks.

"What?" John says, momentarily startled by the question.

"Your favorite song. Everyone has one. And you can tell a lot about a person by their choice of favorite song."

"Okay," John says. "Well, I don't know. I guess 'Falling To Pieces' by Faith No More. It was the first rock song I can remember hearing. At my cousin's house. He was a big metal head. That song was my first real introduction to rock music."

"I don't know that one," Elise says. "My favorite song is 'Crazy.' Patsy Cline. It is just such a perfectly beautiful and sad love song."

"There is no such thing as love," Frankie snickers from off to the side. "Only carnal impulse and quasi-romantic complacency."

"Dude," Gary says. "You don't have to be a douche-bag."

"He's probably a virgin," Taylor says. "So, what is *your* favorite song, boy wonder?"

Frankie turns in his seat to look at her. "I'd have to say 'Bitch,' by the Rolling Stones."

Everyone begins laughing. Frankie grins and turns his attention back to his comic book.

"In your face, sis," Gary says. Taylor flips him off.

"Oh, I'm sorry, Taylor," Gary says. "What's your favorite song?"

"David Bowie. Any song will do." Taylor puts her headphones back on. The Smiths' "Shoplifters Of The World Unite" can be heard very briefly rattling from the tiny speakers.

"I'm gonna go with 'Breaking The Law' by Judas Priest," Gary says. "That song always just pumps me the fuck up."

John looks at Maggie. "What about you?"

"I don't know," Maggie says. "I always liked Queen. 'Keep Yourself Alive.' Yeah. I think that's my favorite song."

Everyone looks at her funny.

"Oh shit," Maggie says. "I forgot, I'm black. Nevermind. I guess my favorite song is 'Baby Got Back.'"

Everyone erupts into laughter.

"Radiohead's 'Creep' has always been my number one song," Wesley says. "It just brings back so many memories, you know."

John catches himself staring at Maggie again. She is so beautiful. He watches her smile. He is trying not to look at Wesley, who is whispering something to her. Then Maggie cuts her eyes to John, as Wesley gets up and heads down the hall. John smiles and nods at Maggie. She smiles back. It's little moments like this that make this entire weekend seem worth it.

Wesley comes back carrying an acoustic guitar. John's guitar. On the back of the guitar is a black label marked GUITAR. Wesley must have found the instrument in John's closet. Sneaky son of a bitch.

"Who wants to hear some old school shit," Wesley says, holding the guitar up for everyone to see.

"Yes!" Maggie says. Gary yells out in agreement.

"John?" Wesley holds the guitar out in John's direction. "Wanna relive some glory days?"

John shakes his head in embarrassment. "I haven't touched that damn thing in a long time, Wesley."

"Quit pouting, bitch," Gary says. "Let's hear some mother fucking Pandora!"

In high school, Wesley and John played in an alternative rock band called Pandora Effect. John played guitar and Wesley was the lead singer. John also did harmony vocals. Sort of an Alice In Chains kind of vibe.

"Come on, bro," Wesley says. "Let's do this. Just one song."

John closes his eyes. Lets out a long sigh. The sight of the guitar did excite him a little. He always loved making music. But the guitar had been a gift from his father years ago. His father had taught him to play it. There were so many mixed memories and emotions attached to the instrument.

"Okay," John finally says. "Hand it over, jackass."

Wesley hands the guitar to John, who begins to check the tuning. Wesley then goes to the kitchen and brings out two chairs from the dining table.

John and Wesley take their seats. John plays a few bars of Nirvana's "Come As You Are" to make sure the guitar is in his preferred tuning, a half-step down.

"What should we play," Wesley asks. "Stone Temple Pilots? We could do 'Plush' or maybe 'Interstate Love Song.'"

"I want to hear 'In The Dead Of Night,'" Maggie says. "I always loved that one."

"In The Dead Of Night" was one of Pandora Effect's original songs. John had written it, as he had most of the band's original compositions. Wesley looks at John, raising his eyebrows in question. John grins and nods, and begins to strum the chords.

And then, John and Wesley begin to sing in unison:

In the dead of night
You feel the angel's bite
Can you stand the pain
Driving you insane
All of the silly words
Your mother always sang
In the dead of night
In the dead of night

In the dead of night
As your love cries out
You can feel your heart
Breaking in your hand
You can say what you like
But the truth will show
In the dead of night
In the dead of night

In the dead of night
You can feel love dying
In the dead of night
You could almost give in
But keep in mind
You have control of your life

And you can do what you like
In the dead of night

(short instrumental bridge)

In the dead of night
You can feel love dying
In the dead of night
You could almost give in
But keep in mind
You have control of your life
And you can do what you like
In the dead of night

The song winds down to a soft end, and everyone in the room begins to applaud. Even Gary's sister had removed her earphones to listen and is smiling.

"That felt good," John thinks to himself. He regrets that the band had split up long ago. Who knows where it could have led. They could have become successful. They could have been playing a concert the night his parents died. His mom and dad would have been at the show, instead up getting crushed head-on by that eighteen-wheeler. John shoves those thoughts aside, and just tries to enjoy the moment for what it is.

Just a happy moment. They are so rare lately. John looks at Maggie. She looks like she has tears in her eyes. John feels his own eyes beginning to water.

Just a happy moment. Enjoy it while it lasts.

Time to take a call from a loyal listener! KMRG, what's up?!

"Hey, Coolhand, uh, I wanna request a song."

Whatchu wanna hear my man?

"Can you play 'Got The Life' by Korn?"

Hey, that's a badass song and all, but you know, this weekend I'm only jamming out songs with storm references of some kind. So what else you got, brother?

"Um.. How about, --what Elise? No. No, I friggin hate that song! (sigh) Fine. Can you play 'No Rain' by Blind Melon?"

There we go. See, you got it now. And that's exactly what every one of us wants this weekend: no rain. Who am I talking to?

"My name is Gary."

What are you up to Gary?

"Me and my friends are having a hurricane party, dude."

Riding out Hurricane Bataille. You guys got some gonads.

"(laughs) Yeah. I guess so."

All right, Gary, thanks for the call. You guys keep safe this weekend, and I'll get that Blind Melon song on for you now, right here on the Mighty Rock Gods, KMRG 99.9 FM, mofos!

"Oh my god," Gary exclaims, holding back laughter. "Do you remember that time John and Wesley broke into that winery and stole like four cases of wine. And John dropped a fucking case and got wine all over his fucking pants. And you fuckers still had like six miles to walk until you got back to Wesley's house!"

Gary is fighting back tears of laughter as he yells out over the music blaring from the radio. Red Hot Chili Peppers. "Naked In The Rain."

"Oh shit," Wesley says, waving his left arm into the air, beer sloshing out of the can of Miller Light he is holding. "That was like the funniest fucking shit ever!"

"Those pants still smell like fucking Merlot," John says.

Frankie is sitting in a recliner reading a trade paperback edition of a recent *The Walking Dead* comic book storyline.

Taylor is sitting on a chair at the dining

table, checking her MySpace messages on a tiny laptop computer. She is viewing her ex-boyfriend Chris' page. Chris dumped Taylor for another girl, Brittani, just three days ago. This is her main incentive for tagging along with her brother for the weekend. She really doesn't need any more drama to worry about right now. Yet here she is, now viewing this bitch Brittani's MySpace page. Staring at her stupid fucking profile picture, hating those perfect fucking dimples and the meticulous eye makeup that looks so fucking awesome. Like a real 1980s goth. Taylor always feels like a poser at a fucking My Chemical Romance concert. Sure, she likes those guys, the singer is fucking cute, but she'd rather look like a dark goddess backstage at a Depeche Mode concert. She sighs, reaches down to turn up the volume on her MP3 player, currently set to a Nine Inch Nails playlist, "Terrible Lie" now playing, to drown out her obnoxious brother and his loud drunken friends.

"Dude," Gary shouts. "We should play a game. A party game!"

"Nah, I fucking hate party games," Wesley says. "I swear I'll fucking die if we have to resort to that shit."

"Well," Gary says, disappointed. "What can we do, then?"

"Here," Elise cuts in, reaching into her purse and pulling out a Ziploc bag full of green, pulpy leaves. "Let's smoke this."

"Fucking A," Gary says, snatching the bag away.

"What kind is that," John asks, leaning in with interest.

"Pure Afghan kush," Elise says.

"Fucking sweet, man," Gary says. "Gimme some papers."

Elise rummages through her purse for a moment. "Shit," she says. "I don't have any."

Gary looks around in disbelief. "Anybody got any papers?"

Everyone shakes their heads, holding out their hands in apologetic gestures.

"Dammit," Gary says. "What about a bong. John! You got a bong, dude?"

"Sorry," John says. "Can you make one?"

"I can't fucking make one," Gary says, looking around desperately for some omen, some sign that hope is not lost. His eyes fall upon Frankie in the recliner.

"Frankie!"

Frankie actually jumps a little at the loud shrill of Gary's voice. He sets his book down nervously. "Yeah? What?"

"Dude," Gary says, calming his voice. "You gotta make us a bong, man."

"Fuck you," Frankie says. "Make your own damn bong."

"We don't know how, man. You're our only hope."

"I really don't want to."

"Taylor!" Gary yells.

Taylor, who had been watching the argument with a little amusement, pulls the tiny earplugs out. "Yeah.."

"Tell Frankie to make us a bong, man. Tell him you'll kick his ass if he don't."

Taylor gets up and walks over to the recliner, staring down with a grin at Frankie. "Make us a fucking bong or I'm gonna kick your fucking ass."

Frankie stares up at Taylor. "What do I get if I do?"

"You get your sad little ass unkicked tonight."

Frankie closes his eyes and sighs. "Son of a bitch.."

Everyone stares at him as he sits up in the recliner.

"You think just because I'm smart that I can just magically construct a bong for you idiotic potheads?"

"You are the smartest dude I know," Gary says, sincerely. "The smartest dude in the whole wide world."

Frankie shakes his head. "Fuck it. Okay. But you better remember this shit the next time I'm getting pushed around."

Frankie proceeds to make a list of items he will need. Gary spends the next forty-five minutes hunting down the items throughout the house, a sort of stoners' scavenger hunt, and finally brings everything listed in a box to Frankie.

"Okay," Frankie says. "Let's see. We have a two-liter water bottle. Hand me that knife."

Gary hands the small pocketknife to Frankie, who uses it to make a small hole about a quarter of the way from the bottom of the empty water bottle. Frankie then takes a plastic Bic pen casing, inserts it into the hole and applies a little J-B Weld to glue it in place.

"Don't get that shit on your fingers, dude," Gary says.

"Fuck off," Frankie snaps back. "I know

what I'm doing."

Frankie then fills about a third of the bottle with crushed chunks of ice. He shoves a bit of heavy duty aluminum foil into the mouth of the bottle, using his fingers to tuck it in, making a small bowl about two inches deep, folding the extra foil on the edge around the outside of the mouth. On the radio, The White Stripes are playing. "Red Rain."

"Where's the needle," Frankie asks. "I asked for a needle."

Gary looks at John questioningly. John just shrugs. "I don't I have any needles."

"Shit," Frankie says.

"Wait," Taylor says. "Here.." She hands over a large safety pin that was uselessly pierced through the thigh of her pants.

"Perfect," Frankie says, taking the safety pin, opening it wide and using the point to poke several holes into the bowl of foil in the mouth of the bottle.

"Here," Frankie says, handing his MacGyvered ice bong to Gary. "Knock yourself out."

"This is so fucking sweet," Gary says, accepting the bong. "Where'd you learn how to do that?"

"High school," Frankie says. "I'd make pipes for the jocks so they wouldn't beat me up like all the other nerds. Worked most of the time."

"Did they smoke up with you," Gary asks.

"Um.. No," Frankie says.

"Well then. Frankie, my man, you are getting first hit."

"Not really my thing," Frankie says nervously.

"Nonsense," Taylor says. "You're toking up with us. And that is final."

Frankie and Taylor stare at each other for a long moment. Finally, Frankie feels his nerve break.

"Fine," he says. "Fill it up."

Gary fills the foil top of the bong with Elise' dark green sweet leaf and lights it while Frankie pulls a long rip from the Bic pen at the bottom. The smoke is cool from the ice, cool on the throat, so smooth going in. Frankie holds the smoke in for a few seconds, then tries to slowly exhale. Instead, a burning sensation coats his entire throat and he begins to cough and gag, pounding on his chest in some strange fit of desperation. Everyone laughs at Frankie. Taylor simply grins, feeling a little admiration for the scrawny dork.

"Son of a bitch!" Frankie says. "I think it

needs a hole near the top. A carburetor."

"Fuck that," Gary says, taking the bong. "Carbs are bad for you. We're on an all natural diet here, man."

Gary relights the weed and takes a rip, leaning back and smiling wide. "Oh sweet baby Jesus. That is some high quality THC."

John watches his friends, waiting for the bong to make it's way to him. He wonders if he should make a label marked BONG. He glances at the TV. The news ticker feed on the bottom of the screen is recapping the Governor's evacuation order for everyone in southwestern Louisiana.

"Tomorrow night," he thinks to himself. *"The storm hits tomorrow night."*

John feels his stomach tighten with that dreadful anticipation when you just know something bad is going to happen. Nauseous. He is feeling very nauseous.

Then, he has the bong in his hand. He takes a hit. The smoke is cool. The pot is strong. All worries vanish from his mind. All that remains is the sound of laughter. And Billy Joel's "Stormfront" playing on the radio.

Okay guys. I gotta tell you, at first I thought the excitement over this weekend would be enough to keep me pumping all the way through, but I have to say I'm already feeling the burn. I am exhausted. And we're just getting started. We haven't even gotten to the craziness yet. There is so much violence and devastation coming up, and I really don't want to think about it. This is going to be a long couple of nights for everyone. But I want to reassure everyone, I'm sticking with you. I will be here if you need me. If you're scared and just want to call in and talk, that's cool. The regular format for this weekend is relaxed a little. I can do pretty much whatever I want. I'm the boss for now. It's just me and a couple of station helpers, Trey and Sage, I want to thank you guys for hanging with me, pushing all those buttons and keeping the hot chocolate flowing for me (laughs). And I want to thank all of you out there who are rocking out with us. I'm gonna play one of my favorite songs right now. The Who. "Call Me Lightning." So keep those dials tuned right here to KMRG 99.9 FM. We are your Mighty Rock Gods, and you know we effin rule!

John lies in his bed, but cannot sleep. He is unsure if it is the thoughts racing through his mind, some good, some bad. Excitement over seeing his friends again, after so long. Nervousness over how the weekend is going to turn out.

Maybe it is the sounds coming from the guest bedroom directly above him. The room where Wesley and Maggie are staying. The room where they are enthusiastically making love right now.

John stares up at the ceiling. Just listening. The slight creak of the bed's springs. The light thump of the headboard hitting the wall at a steady beat. Maggie's long, slow, drawn out moans, interrupted by sudden high-pitched squeaks and *oh gods*. John pictures her, naked, her dark skin in the moonlight. Black nipples hard and glistening with sweat and saliva. Her crotch, is it shaved? He's not sure. He imagines it is. He is sure it is warm and wet, still a little tight since she is in athletically good shape.

"Oh god Oh god Oh god Oooohhh," she screams as the thumping of the headboard gets harder. Louder.

John is hard beneath his covers, and he is struggling not to grip himself. He tries to block out the sounds coming from above. Tries to think of something else. Anything else.

At a near breaking point, John jumps out of bed and heads for the bathroom. In his medicine cabinet he finds a bottle of sleeping pills. Stuck to the outside of the bottle is a black label that reads SLEEP. A generic version of one of those highly praised dream-inducing brands with the trippy TV commercials. Glowing neon butterflies lulling people to slumber with the slightest touch. *Scary fucking bug*, John has thought. He tosses four pills down his throat, washing them down with a handful of water from the sink faucet. There are other bottles, with other black labels. Some read SMILE. Some read LIGHT. Others say things like WORK and THINK and FORGET. John ignores these other bottles and closes the medicine cabinet.

Back out in the hall, John becomes distracted by the sound of uncomfortable moans and weeping from the guest bedroom across from the bathroom. The room where Gary and his girlfriend are staying.

John walks up to the door, cautiously, to listen. He hears the girl, Elise, groan in agony, and Gary telling her to shut up. John always knew that Gary had a bit of a violent side, but he'd have never suspected Gary would abuse a girlfriend. John grits his teeth, readies himself, and throws the door open, bursting into the room.

"What the fuck is going on in here!" John yells.

It takes John a moment to adjust to what he is seeing. Elise is practically nude, on the bed, on her hands and knees, with a ball gag in her mouth. Her wrists are bound together with leather cuffs. Her legs are spread apart, and there is a metal bar extended between them, attached with leather straps to her lower thighs. Gary is on his knees behind her, wearing a black leather bondage mask with a zipper mouth. He is also wearing a black leather vest, and black leather gloves that go up to his elbows. Below the waist he is nude, a massive erection standing upright. Gary has a small whip, a fucking horse crop, and has apparently been whacking Elise on her behind, her ass cheeks glowing red with thin criss-crossing lines.

"Dude," Gary says. "What's up, man?"

"Um," John says, then goes silent. He is at a total loss for words. Finally he just bows his head, raises one hand up as in an act of surrender, and slowly back out of the room.

John shuts the bedroom door, and listens for a moment. The sounds of whipping and crying start again.

"Jesus fucking Christ," John says with a grin as he walks away.

John goes into the kitchen to get a glass of orange juice. It has always helped him sleep at night. It's probably his favorite flavor in the world. His favorite smell. Even his shampoo and conditioner are citrus-scented.

He walks back out through the living room, and in the light of the TV he notices that Gary's sister Taylor is laying beside Frankie, the nerd lord, on the couch. Her back is to him and they are dry humping the crap out of each other. John is sufficiently in the shadows and is confident he can not be seen. But still, why? Taylor seemed to hate Frankie. And the sentiment had seemed to be mutual. Unless it was all a ruse. Maybe Taylor is into dorky guys, but doesn't like to admit it. Taylor is moaning, steadily and forcefully.

"Can I stick it in you," Frankie whispers.

"Don't be gross, asshole," Taylor coldly whispers back. She then starts thrusting her backside harder into Frankie, who grips her breasts, burying his face into her shoulder and neck.

John wonders why he is feeling so doomed to catch everybody exploring their lusts tonight. What horrible sin has he committed, that this is the punishment he should receive. Perhaps it's all because he invited everyone here in the first place. Questioning his own intentions, and then realizing he was getting hard in his boxers, John creeps away back to his bedroom.

Back in bed, John stares up at the ceiling.

35

The Wesley and Maggie sex storm up above is apparently over. He missed the big climax. But there's another storm coming and he is beginning to seriously wonder if his house is strong enough to take it.

And then, he wonders if he is strong enough to take it as well.

Good morning, Vietnam! Coolhand Madman here, and I am wired and tired and totally fired UP! and this is the day, this is it, before today is over Hurricane Bataille is gonna open up a big wet can of crazy whoop-ass on all of us. And I'm ready. I say bring it on. I apologize to everyone for the programmed song list earlier this morning, but I had to get a few hours of shut eye. So for those of you who may have tried to call in, I'm very sorry about that. Give us a try now. Or later today. Let me know what you're doing today. You packing up to leave at the last minute? Boarding up those windows? Getting crunk and drunk and gotta have that funk waiting on that Cat-5 to drop down? I'm all ears, and all mouth, and I say let there be rock! Here's Duran Duran, "The Sound Of Thunder," on your Mighty Rock Gods KMRG 99.9 FM!

The smell of grilling meat fills the air. Steam rises up from hot coals as bloody juice and fat drips down from tenderized twelve-ounce sirloins and Ballpark hotdogs.

Gary is chasing a stray kitten around the backyard. His sister Taylor is sitting on a lawn chair, listening to The Dresden Dolls on her MP3 player, "Necessary Evil" is the song currently playing, while reading author Collin Monroe's nonfiction book *The Devil's Lodge: The Louisiana Hunters Cult and Other True Mysteries.* Elise is sprawled out on a large beach blanket in shorts and a yellow and pink bikini top, working on a somewhat elusive golden tan.

John and Wesley are at the grill. Wesley is forming ground buffalo meat into hamburger patties. John is flipping the steaks over, watching Maggie as she heads into the house.

"Where is Gary's friend?" John asks.

"The brainiac," Wesley says, smiling. "Probably inside reading his comic books or reformulating quantum physics or some shit. He was trying to explain string theory to us on the ride in. I was this close to stopping the van and theoretically stringing him up from a fucking tree."

John gives a weak chuckle. He looks up at the sky. There are more clouds than yesterday. But nothing that would indicate a hurricane was close at hand.

"You think it's gonna get bad tonight?" Wesley asks.

"Yeah," John says, turning his concentration back to the grill. "I think it's gonna get real bad."

John forks the hotdogs off the grill, setting them aside on a platter. "Did you bring out the sausage links?"

"Shit," Wesley says. "No, sorry. My hands were full."

"Here," John says, handing the long fork to Wesley. "Watch the grill. I'll go get the other food."

John wipes his hands on a towel and heads for the backdoor of his house. Inside, he goes into the kitchen. He takes two packages of sausage links from the fridge, as well as some long asparagus and an extra bottle of barbecue sauce.

Arms full, he turns away from the fridge to walk away and collides with Maggie who seems to appear from nowhere. John drops everything he's carrying, the cold goods scattering all over the kitchen floor.

"Fuck!" Maggie shouts, laughing. "I'm so sorry, John."

"It's fine," John says as he and Maggie drop down to their knees to pick up the food. Maggie stares at John, who seems to be avoiding eye contact.

"Are you all right?" she asks.

"What? Yeah. Sure. I'm fine."

"You've been acting weird all day."

"It's nothing.."

"It doesn't seem like nothing."

John sighs. "I would really rather not talk about it."

Maggie reaches out and grabs his shoulder. "Hey. We've been friends forever. There shouldn't be anything that we can't talk about."

"It's about you."

"Me?"

"You and Wesley."

"Oh." Maggie pulls her hand away. "Okay."

"I just don't really get it," John says, finally looking at her.

"He asked me out," Maggie says. "So we went out. We kept it up."

"Do you love him?"

"Maybe we shouldn't be having this conversation.."

"Do you *love* him, Maggie?"

"John.." Maggie goes silent for a moment, swallowing hard. "Yes. Sure I do. Is that some sort of problem for you?"

"No.."

"Well then why don't you just tell me what's on your mind."

John sits in silence. Gathering his thoughts. He is so nervous. Terrified. He has never been this uncomfortable talking to Maggie before. Tears begin to well in his eyes.

"I miss them, Maggie. Mom and Dad. I literally knew them my entire life. And then they were just gone. And I'm okay with that now, mostly. The only other person I knew that long was you. And to be honest, I miss you too. So much."

"I'm right here, John." She grabs his

shoulder again.

"No. I mean I *miss* you."

John stares hard at Maggie. She stares back. She had been wondering when this would happen.

"Are you jealous of Wesley?"

"Jealousy has got nothing to do with it," John says, his voice almost cracking. "I love you, Maggie. I always have."

Maggie takes her hand from his shoulder once more, and stares down at the floor.

"But I missed my chance, didn't I?" John asks.

Maggie reaches up to wipe tears from her eyes. "You," she starts, struggling with the words. "You are a fucking jerk."

"Maggie.."

"No! John.. You have no fucking right to do this. You can not just throw this shit on me. Not now. I'm with Wesley. We are really getting along. We are really enjoying being together. So, yeah, you missed your fucking chance, asshole."

"I'm sorry," John says as Maggie stands up, crying.

"Don't," she says. "Just don't."

A noise draws their attention away. Frankie is standing at the doorway between the kitchen and the living room. Everyone stares at each other in silence.

"Is the food about ready?" Frankie finally nervously asks.

"Yeah," John says. Maggie walks past Frankie, heading for the bathroom. John just watches her. He missed his chance. He knows that now. But there is always a second chance. He'd heard that somewhere.

"Is everything okay?" Frankie surprisingly asks.

"Well," John says, staring out the open back door, and the clouds in the sky which are growing darker by the hour. "Things could be worse."

Ladies and gentlemen, loyal listeners, things are officially about to get worse. Up to this point things have been pretty calm. But ten minutes ago, at 11:38 PM local time, Hurricane Bataille made landfall, on the Louisiana coast about fifteen miles east of Grand Chenier. The storm is so big, that it is covering ground from the Texas border to the Atchafalaya Bay. This is one massive storm, people. Now we've been having a little trouble with our broadcast transmitters. The wind has been picking up, and it's starting to get really noisy out there. This is it. This is probably your last chance. If you get out now, you might be able to get out of the area. We know the roads are getting backed up a good bit, so it has been a slow evacuation, but it's going rather smooth. That's what we're hearing from our sources with the state emergency officials. I repeat, Hurricane Bataille is on land. If you are listening to this, then you are certainly in the area that will be most affected. So keep your radio dialed to us, KMRG 99.9 FM. We'll be your constant source of information, as always, on anything going on with this storm. Be careful people. This is the part where things start to get rough. But I'm sticking with you. I'll be here for you. Here's some

more music, to keep you rocking through the madness. The Doors. "Riders On The Storm."

Everyone is gathered around the TV. Staring at the images on the screen. Cypress trees thrashing back and forth. Storm surges pushing water from the Gulf, sending violent waves crashing into the coast. John looks over at Maggie, who is doing her best to pretend she does not notice. But she can't take it. She glances over, making eye contact. There is such sadness in both of their eyes. Such longing. John wants to just reach out and hold her. And honestly, so does Maggie.

All concentration is shattered by a sudden unexpected knocking at the front door.

"Dude," Gary says, looking toward John. "You expecting somebody?"

John just stares at the front door. Another round of knocks, harder this time.

"I guess I'll get it," Wesley says, getting up and walking across the room to the locked and latched front door. He unlocks it, but leaves the chain latched. Outside the rain is pouring. The wind is pretty strong, though not nearly as bad as what was being shown on TV. Light from the house seeps out through the barely opened door, illuminating the face of an unknown man. There is a woman standing beside him, but her face is hidden by the darkness outside.

"Are friends electric?" the man asks low, barely audible.

"Excuse me?" Wesley asks, straining to hear.

"Hey buddy," the man says. "We ran off the road about a mile up. We need to use a phone."

Wesley just stares at the man, then notices another man peering out from behind his shoulder, his right eye illuminated vaguely.

"Who is it, Wesley?" Gary asks.

Wesley turns and looks at John. "Some people want to use the phone."

"It's really pouring down out here, buddy," the man says. "Have a little human compassion."

John walks up to the door, closes it, unlatches the chain, and opens the door again. He looks out at the man and woman, fully illuminated now. The man behind them still faintly hidden in shadow.

"This your house?" the man asks.

"Yeah," John answers.

"It looks nice."

"Thanks."

John and the man stare at each other for a long moment. "Can we come inside?" the man finally asks.

John hesitates for a moment, turns to look at his friends, making eye contact with Maggie, who is watching with keen interest. John then opens the door all the way. "Sure. Of course. Come on in."

"Thanks, friend." The man enters the house, pulling the woman's hand, she in turn pulling the hand of the other man until they are all three inside the house, dripping wet, creating a large wet puddle on the hardwood floor.

"We were, um, trying to get to Lafayette, using mostly the rural highways. Trying to avoid the interstate," the man says, taking his waterproof backpack off and setting it on the floor. "My name's Scott." He extends his hand to John.

"I'm John."

"Good to meet you, John. This is my girlfriend Claire, and her little brother Daniel."

John says hi to both. Claire smiles with a wink. Daniel just stares down at the floor. Scott looks around the room at the others. "We interrupting a little get-together?"

"Hurricane party," John says.

"No shit? Ballsy. You guys must be the only people in this area who didn't evacuate."

"These are my friends," John says. "Gary and his girlfriend Elise. Gary's roommate Frankie. Gary's sister Taylor. And you've met Wesley."

"Sup," Wesley says. He never sat back down after answering the door, and he is watching the new arrivals with suspicion.

"And over there," John says, motioning back towards the couch. "That is Maggie."

"Hi Maggie," Scott says with a wide smile. "She your girlfriend?"

"No," John says.

"She's with me," Wesley says.

"My bad, buddy," Scott says, the smile never fading.

Wesley turns to get the cordless house phone from the kitchen. He picks it up, hits a button and puts it to his ear. "There is no dial tone. The lines must be down."

Everyone checks their cell phones. No signals.

"You are more than welcome to stay for a bit," John says to Scott.

"I don't want to impose," Scott says.

"Not a concern. I can't send you back out into that storm."

"Thanks, friend."

Claire speaks up. "Is it all right if we get changed?"

"Sure," John says. "The bathroom is down the hall. First door on the right."

Claire says thanks, and the three strangers take their backpacks and head to the bathroom. Wesley watches until they close the door, then he grabs John by the arm forcefully.

"What the fuck, dude? You don't know these people."

"I can't just turn them away," John says. "It's my house, and I think it's fine."

"I don't like the way they look. They smell like trouble."

"You think everybody looks like trouble," John says, grinning.

"You see that skinny kid with them,"

Wesley says. "He was staring at Maggie. Creepy-like shit."

"You're overreacting."

"I don't overreact when it comes to her, John."

John nods at Wesley, and they just stare at each other. After a moment, the bathroom door opens and the three strangers come back out to the living room.

"Thanks again," Scott says to John.

"No problem," John says. Wesley goes to sit back down beside Maggie.

"It's chilly in here," Claire says, stretching her arms back wide. Her braless breasts pushing out against the cotton fabric of her Dwight Yoakam tank top, erect nipples pointing out like tiny bullets. Her arms are covered with tattoos. A few more are visible on her hips, and there may be more toward her crotch. Her ripped up blue jeans expose more tattoos on her legs. Frankie stares at her, his eyes simultaneously fixated on the Boba Fett belt buckle, and the protruding nipples. Claire catches Frankie staring, and grins. Frankie looks away, embarrassed.

"Would anyone like a drink," John asks.

"Beers are fine," Scott says, while fingering a small red stain on his Hellfire Grub t-shirt.

"Three beers," John says, heading for the kitchen.

The three strangers stand in the center of the room, looking at John's friends, who all stare back. Wesley especially, who does not trust these people at all. Scott is looking at Maggie, who takes a moment to notice. When she does, he winks and smiles. She blushes and grins, turns her head toward the kitchen to watch John getting the beers. This makes Scott smile wider. He scans the room, looking at everyone, and as John returns with the cans of Bud Light, Scott holds in a slight laugh as he thinks to himself *"Which one of these fucking idiots will be the first to die."*

You know, I hate to be this blunt, but it needs to be said. If you are still out there, sitting at home listening to us, hearing that rain pound against the side of your house, then it is too late. You're not going anywhere. The winds are picking up drastically. It's about to get pretty violent. Just giving you a little warning. But I'm sure you knew that already. You wouldn't be here if you weren't expecting things to get a little crazy. You probably get off on that sort of thing. Well, I don't think you'll be disappointed. We're about to cross over that threshold, where we go from waiting for the terror to start, to waiting for the horror to end. This is it. No turning back. Nowhere to go but straight into the arms of Hell. Buckle up, kids. It's about to get bumpy. So let's turn it up with the ultimate rockers, Kiss. "God Of Thunder" on KMRG 99.9 FM.

"So where are you guys from," Gary asks the new guests.

"I am originally from New Orleans," Scott says. "But I lived in Natchez, Mississippi, for a good ten years or so. I've been in Lake Charles for the last couple of years."

"Daniel and I are from Lafayette," Claire says. "I have friends with a big house there. That's where we were heading."

"Looks like you're not going to get there tonight," Elise says.

"Looks like," Scott agrees, grinning at her.

"I'll be back in a sec," Maggie says, standing up. "Little girls' room."

A little drunk, she heads down the hall to the bathroom. Everyone continues talking, not noticing when Claire's brother Daniel slowly stands up and heads down the hall.

Maggie has neglected to shut the bathroom door all the way, and Daniel pushes it open a little. His eyes fall on her just as she stands up from the toilet to wipe herself. His eyes lock on the dark black lips of her vulva just as she realizes he is there. Startled, she pulls up her pants quickly.

"I saw your privates," Daniel says. "Do you want to see mine?"

He begins to unzip his pants.

"Wesley!" Maggie screams.

Wesley comes running from the living room and jerks Daniel away from the door.

"What the fuck, you fucking pervert!"

Soon enough, everyone else is in the hall, to witness the commotion.

Claire pulls Daniel away from Wesley. "What are you doing, Daniel. You trying to get us all in trouble here!"

Wesley tries to grab Daniel again.

"Fuck off," Claire shouts. "I can handle him."

Wesley goes to console Maggie, who is very disturbed and upset.

"I want them to leave," she says. "Tell John

to make them leave. I can't stay in a house with that goddamned pervert."

"Look, bitch," Claire snaps. "My brother's not a pervert. He's just a little slow. He doesn't know any better."

"Your brother is a fucking freak!" Wesley yells.

"Calm down everybody," Scott says.

Daniel starts to laugh to himself, rubbing the erection in his pants, staring at Maggie.

"You sick little fuck," Wesley says. "I swear to god, I'm going to fuck him up."

"Please," Scott says. "We need to calm down."

"I'll hold him down," Gary says. "You kick his ass."

"You touch him and I will fucking kill you," Claire says.

"Bitch," Wesley says. "You need to shut the fuck up right now!"

A DEAFENING SHOT RINGS OUT!

Everyone stops arguing and looks over at Scott, who is holding a pistol. He has fired a single shot up into the ceiling. Bits of dust floating down around him.

"Now," Scott says. "That's better."

Everyone is silent for a moment. Daniel just grins to himself.

"What's with the gun, bro," Wesley says, holding Maggie close.

"It's for protection," Scott says.

"From what?" Wesley asks.

Claire puts a gun of her own against the back of Wesley's head.

"From all the freaks that come out during a storm," she says.

Everyone remains silent. The only sound is the rain and the wind whistling outside. Finally, Scott says "It's too fucking quiet. I thought this was supposed to be a party."

No one says anything. They just stare.

"Let's have some mother fucking fun," Scott says.

That was "Butterflies And Hurricanes" by Muse. How about we open up that request line. We've had a ton of people calling in tonight. I'm surprised. There's more of you riding out Hurricane Bataille than I would have expected. Hello, this is Coolhand Madman--

"Am I on the air?"

You are, my lady? Who is this?

"Katryna."

Katryna, that's a morbidly appropriate name to have this weekend.

"Yeah, well, my name is spelled with a Y."

Duly noted. You hanging in there for this wicked weather?

"Yeah. I didn't really feel like leaving. I have animals, and it would have been too hard to get them all out of here in my little car."

That's great. I hope you're holding up okay.

"Yeah. I've been through this all before. I think I can handle it."

You want to request a song?

"Yeah. I wanted to request something by The Romantics, but I don't think they have any weather songs (laughs)."

Not that I know of. We can check around though.

"So how about Prince. 'Purple Rain.'"

Hey. You're a real live 80s kind of chick.

"Yeah (laughs)."

My kind of chick, Katryna. Sure. We'll hook you up with some Prince. Just tell everybody who your favorite radio station is.

"I absolutely love the Mighty Rock Gods, KMRG 99.9 FM! WOO HOO!"

John and his friends are sitting in the living room. No one says a word. John looks at Daniel, who sits in a chair with a pistol at the ready.

"Don't accidentally shoot one of them, Danny Boy!" Scott says.

Daniel laughs. On the radio, "Weather Bell" by The The is playing. Scott and Claire are dancing together. The crazier they dance, the more Daniel laughs. Scott begins groping on Claire, and Daniel's laughter begins to weaken. Scott pulls Claire close and kisses her, deep.

"NO!" Daniel yells and, distraught, runs out of the room, rushing down the hallway.

Claire ends her dance with Scott, and heads down the hall, calling out her brother's name.

Scott sits down with his gun, staring at his captives.

"So," Scott says. "You guys having a good time this weekend?"

No one responds. They just briefly look up at Scott, and after making eye contact with his gun, they look away.

"Not feeling talkative, eh?"

Still no response. Scott notices the book that Taylor has been gripping in her lap like a security blanket.

"Whatchu reading?"

Taylor just looks away.

"Come on," Scott says. "Don't be shy. Let me see."

Taylor tosses the book in his direction. Scott picks it up, and frowns when he reads the cover.

"*The Devil's Lodge*. By fucking Collin Monroe. Arrogant son of a bitch."

Scott begins laughing to himself.

"This book is bullshit, you know that right? This fucking cop, he wrote this shit about a devil worshipping cult in the woods, all kinds of crazy Satanic shit. But he don't know what the fuck he's talking about. Some people up that way even threatened to sue him, saying he made a bunch of shit up to exploit their misery. And he *did* make a bunch of shit up. And I should know, because I was there. I know what really happened. And it wasn't like that. Satan ain't got shit on what was going on up there. It was some fucked up crazy ass shit. And I've been trying to get away from that shit for two years now. And this damn book just seems to keep popping up all over the fucking place."

Scott throws the book back at Taylor.

"You should be reading *Twilight* or some shit. Not this pack of lies."

Everyone sits in uncomfortable silence. No one knows what the hell Scott has been rambling on about. Except for Taylor. She had been reading the book. It's all about a secretive cult that was based in a hunting lodge in the rural town of Monterey, Louisiana. There were a number of missing persons cases, and everything led to this lodge. But the place had been burned to the ground by the time authorities arrived. There were underground rooms filled with altars, makeshift prison cells, human remains, occult contraband, even a deep pit with a drugged up deer, it's antlers filed down into sharp points which it, supposedly, used to kill victims who were tossed down into the pit with it. A few suspects' bodies were found, either burned or gouged to death by an unknown assailant. Some victims had been torn apart, body parts scattered throughout the property and the surrounding woods. The author of the book, Collin Monroe, was a local deputy during the events described in the book. He estimates that dozens of other possible suspects escaped and are still on the loose today. That it all ties into the Illuminati and the Masons, Satanic secret societies, an underworld black market for cannibalism, and other outrageous claims. It is truly one of the craziest true crime mysteries to ever come out of Louisiana. The case has never been successfully solved. And now, hearing Scott admit that he was involved in all that madness, Taylor is feeling very worried. She doesn't know if he was telling the truth or not, but she has goosebumps, and cannot seem to stop her hands from trembling.

"I need to go to the bathroom," John says nervously.

"Piss in your shoe," Scott says.

"I don't have to piss."

"Then take a shit in your fucking shoe," Scott says, bursting into laughter. "I'm just fucking with you, man. Go ahead. But no funny stuff."

On his way to the bathroom John hears voices coming from his bedroom. He goes to look through the crack in the open door. Claire and Daniel are sitting on the bed, their backs to the door. Claire is trying to console her brother, who is crying.

"Do you like that girl out there," she asks. "The one from the bathroom."

Daniel nods his head. "She's a real pretty nigger."

"Now what did I tell you? We don't say that word. It's hateful. You don't like it when people call you retard, do you?"

Daniel, looks down in shame. Shakes his head. "No."

"It's the same thing. We don't use hateful words, okay?"

"Okay."

"Good. Now, did she make your privates get hard?"

"Mmhm," he says, excitedly nodding.

"Poor thing. If I make your privates hard again, will you stop crying for me?"

Daniel just looks at her, and then nods. She reaches over, unzips his pants, and begins to play with him.

"You know I love you Daniel. Big sister would never do anything to hurt you."

"I love you too," he says, then Claire leans down to put her face into his lap.

John backs away from the door, clearly disturbed, and slowly heads back towards the bathroom.

Man. The rain is really coming down out there. If this station had a tin roof, I could really pass out right now. I'm so tired. I can not wait for this night to be over. What's that..? Yeah. That's a badass song. Okay, let's get it up. Trey, my engineer, he wants to hear "Rain" by The Cult, and I am more than happy to oblige. I hadn't thought of that one. I love The Cult. One of my favorite bands. You know another song we haven't played? "The Rain Song." By Led Zeppelin. I know! We'll have to play that one later. And I thought we were running out of storm songs. I swear, I think we've played Iron Maiden's "Lightning Strikes Twice" about seven times already. I know, it's a cool song. But we need to expand our playlist some more, you know. I wanted to play "Rainy Day Mushroom" by Strawberry Alarm Clock, but I think our 60s acid rock collection needs a little updating. I couldn't find it. I tried to download it, but our internet is down. Anyway, yeah, The Cult. Here you go, guys. You're listening to the Mighty Rock Gods, KMRG at 99.9 FM.

"Party games are just the fucking best," Scott says. With his gun, he forces everyone to sit in a circle on the floor. He finds a half-empty bottle of vodka and finishes it off, guzzling the burning liquid down his throat, and sets the bottle on the floor in the center of the circle.

"Spin the bottle," Scott says, joining the circle. Claire sits as well. "I always loved this fucking game. How about you guys?"

"Can I go to the bathroom," Elise suddenly asks.

"No," Scott says.

"But you let John go, why can't I?"

"You know, there's just something about the guy," Scott says. "I can't say what it is. I just like him. And besides, I'm a guest in his house, and I didn't want to be rude."

Scott looks at Wesley. "How about you spin first, pretty boy."

Hesitantly, Wesley reaches out to grasp the bottle. He gives it a meager clockwise spin. When the bottle comes to a stop, it is pointing at Elise.

"Oh, don't let your buddy get jealous," Scott says, laughing, pointing his gun at Wesley. "Pucker up, lovebirds."

Wesley leans over and kisses Elise lightly on the lips. Quite obviously the most unromantic kiss in the history of kisses.

"What the fuck was that," Scott says. "I know you can fucking do better than that, padre."

Wesley leans over to kiss Elise again. This time, they both open themselves up, practically devouring each others tongues.

"Here we are now," Scott says, smiling. "Entertain us."

"I'm next," Claire excitedly squeals. She grabs the bottle, spins it counterclockwise. The bottle stops, pointing at Elise.

"You are popular tonight," Claire says, leaning over, grabbing Elise' face with her hands, forcing her tongue into her unwilling mouth.

"That's fucking hot, babe," Scott says.

Claire pulls away from the kiss, licks her lips, and smiles at Scott.

"Can I play, too?" Daniel nervously says from his chair off to the side.

"No," Scott says. "This is a game for grownups."

Daniel gets a sad disappointed look on his face. Scott just laughs. Claire gets slightly irritated by Scott, but she pushes the feeling away.

"You're up, boss-man," Scott says to John. John just stares at the bottle for a moment, then slowly reaches out to give it a spin.

As if by some perverse miracle, the bottle comes to a stop aimed at Maggie. John and Maggie stare at each other.

"What are you guys waiting for," Scott says. "Mother fucking Christmas?"

John feels frozen. He has never felt this nervous in his life. Maggie then reaches for him. She kisses him deep. John kisses back.

"That's what the fuck I'm talking about!" Scott shouts. "Now we're having fun!"

Wesley stares at Maggie and John. The kiss seems to go on a few moments longer than necessary. When they finally release themselves from their tongue embrace, they stare into each others eyes. Maggie, with a hint of a grin on her face, sits back down. The grin quickly vanishes, as she seems to remember the situation that everyone is in.

"Okay, iron head," Scott says to Gary. "You're the next contestant."

Gary quickly grabs the bottle and spins, trying to get it over with quickly. The bottle comes to rest aimed at Scott.

"You're just not my type, pal," Scott says, laughing. "But I'll pass you on to Claire."

"Sexy MF," Claire says, crawling across the empty space between them and grabs Gary, kissing him with no small amount of lust. She breaks the kiss off abruptly, with a disappointed look.

"The twit over there was a better kisser," she says, laughing, pointing at Elise. "Let's try that again."

Claire kisses Gary again, reaching down to grip his crotch. She tells him to stand up. He does. She unzips his pants and slips her hand down his boxer shorts. Gary tries to twitch away, but Claire has his cock gripped firmly in her hand. His erection comes to life easily, and Claire leans in to give him a blowjob.

"Oh babe," Scott says, grabbing his own crotch. "You are such a fucking tease."

Elise tries not to watch, but she can't help it. Her eyes linger on Gary's cock, disappearing and reappearing over and over from the depths of Claire's open, slobbering mouth. She feels wetness in her crotch, and she tries to fight the sensation. But it's unmanageable. It's making her horny.

Claire strokes Gary's cock, and she can feel the muscles begin to contract. She knows the end is coming, and she grabs Gary's hip with her free hand, and turns him to the side, giving his cock that final stroke that releases his cloudy man juice, which rushes out in a warm stream. Frankie, who is sitting next to them, has no time to react. The white lava splashes his face with a wet splat. Frankie moans out in surprise. Claire and Scott begin laughing hysterically.

"You fucking bitch," Frankie yells, wiping the cum from his eyes.

Claire leans over to Frankie, and grabs his crotch. "Hey, I think the dork here kinda liked getting shot in the face!" Laughs. "Do you like pecker milk, faggot?"

Frankie pushes her away. "Leave me alone, you fucking psycho." He is on the verge of tears.

Claire slaps him hard across the face. "Now you listen up, faggot. I don't think you have a firm understanding of the chain of command here."

She climbs onto Frankie's lap. She grinds her crotch against him. "Do you want to stick it in my ass, pretend I'm your buddy over there? He's your roommate right? Tell me, how many times did you stay up, pretending to sleep, just to watch him come in late, undress and get into bed, or drying himself off after a shower. You watched him, didn't you? You little pervert. (laughs) You wanted to rub his muscular chest, and caress his wrinkly nut sack in your hands, take that cock in your mouth. But you were scared, because, let's admit it, your buddy - Gary, right? - he's got a huge fucking cock. I'm lucky I took care of my gag reflex years ago or I would have blown chunks all over his fucking balls."

Frankie has a sudden violent spasm of vomit, which soaks Claire down in warm bile and partially dissected food.

"YOU SICK LITTLE FUCK!"

"I'm sorry," Frankie says, crying.

"Don't be sorry baby," Claire says. "I thought you was just a faggy boy. I didn't know you was a vomit freak."

Claire unzips Frankie's pants, pulls out his hard little prick and slips it inside of her. She grinds on top of him, moaning and laughing, while he sobs. She reaches up and shoves a finger down her throat, forcing herself to choke. Claire gags for a moment, then finally spews hot filth out of her mouth into Frankie's face. She orgasms, and laughs frenetically.

"You are a real madwoman," Scott says. "Why don't you two go get washed up."

Claire gets up, laughing, and drags Frankie down the hall to the bathroom.

"Man, this night is turning out to be more fun that I initially imagined," Scott says. "I'm an orgasm addict!"

Scott begins laughing loudly, rudely, purposefully obnoxious, into everyone's faces.

"You guys are a fucking trip, I swear to god."

After a few minutes, Claire and Frankie come back from the bathroom. "Deflowered, defiled, and rehabilitated," Claire says, making Frankie sit back down.

"This really is so much fun," Scott says. "But you know what's even more fun?"

He stands up, staring at everyone.

"Well?" Scott says, but no one answers. He goes to the radio. "I'll show you."

He turns the radio up louder. "Rain" by Concrete Blonde is playing. He starts to dance a little. He points his gun at Taylor. "Get up. Come here."

She hesitates, but staring at the gun, she knows there is no use in fighting it. So she gives in. Scott wraps his arms around her, lovingly. Dancing slow.

"Keep your electric eyes on me, babe," Scott whispers to Taylor.

Claire smiles watching them. Scott forces Taylor to strip down to her underwear, and beckons Claire to come over. Claire comes up to dance with Taylor. Scott backs away to watch as Claire gropes on her a little, kissing on her. Claire's hands delicately explore Taylor's breasts. They move down to the black and pink stripped panties. A hand slips down the front, a finger quickly slides down and up between the soft folds of Taylor's young vagina. Frankie stares with a little shame, but he can't deny he is fascinated by Taylor's body. Taylor is soon handed back to Scott.

Scott dances with Taylor some more, with her back to his chest. He runs his hands down her body, to her crotch so that he can molest her as well. He pulls his hand away quickly.

"Look at this now!" Scott says. "The bitch went and pissed herself." He points to her panties, which are soaked, and her legs have fresh lines of piss running down. "That's nasty, baby. But kinky too."

Scott laughs, and pulls Taylor to him tight. He dances more erratically with her. Claire embraces them both, dancing away.

Gary has been watching Daniel, who can't take his eyes off the dancing. Gary looks at the gun in Daniel's hand. The gears inside Gary's mind begin turning.

Scott is kissing on Taylor, and pulls her panties down below her hips. He starts to molest her. "We're gonna have us some real fun now," he says. "Hey, Danny Boy. You want to come over here and lick her pissy little pussy?"

Daniel beams wide, excited, and Gary takes his chance. He rushes at Daniel, grabbing the gun away and points it at Daniel's head.

"Let my sister go!" Gary yells.

"Okay, Superman," Scott says. "No need to get your tights in a wad. There's no heroes here, man. Just villains and victims. And don't you go thinking you know the difference between the two."

Claire laughs. Scott lets Taylor go, and she goes to Gary's side, cowering against him.

"Now you're gonna let us all go," Gary says.

"No," Scott says. "I don't think so."

"I'll blow his fucking brains out, man," Gary says, forcing the gun harder against Daniel's head.

"No. You won't," Scott says, raising his gun and pointing it at Gary. "Do you really think I'd let that fucking retard handle a loaded gun?"

Gary gets a slightly confused look on his

face, and glances towards his gun. In this instant, Scott fires his gun, hitting Gary in the chest. Taylor screams and backs away as Gary collapses to the floor. Elise jumps up from the floor and runs to Gary. Daniel grabs the gun and points it at Elise, who cuddles Gary's body.

"Go ahead, Danny Boy. Shoot her. Then you can fuck her," Scott says.

Elise looks up. "You said his gun wasn't loaded."

"I lied," Scott says, with a wink.

Taylor looks at Scott. "You are a sick, fucking monster."

Scott rushes at her, slapping her hard across the face. Taylor falls down to floor, sobbing, holding herself.

"Do you see now?!" Scott says. "Do you fucking see? There is no stopping me. Things are only going to get worse for you motherfuckers. Do what thou wilt shall be the whole of the law. And my law is chaos, motherfuckers. My law is decadence. I'm a street-talking cheetah with a heart full of napalm. I'm a new world order libertine. I am God in this house. I am the Devil himself. I am so many fucking things, so many horrible motherfucking things, but I am not a monster, little girl. I have seen monsters. I have seen things you cannot even begin to imagine. There are things in this world we are not supposed to know about. Shit that I should not know about. But I do know. I have seen. I have seen the fucking horns. I have stared into the fucking eyes of horror. I have looked, and I have seen. And now, you will see. I am going to show you hell. I am going to show you pure evil. I am going to show you things you will never forget."

Scott, dripping with sweat and saliva, looks around at the frightened captives. Even Claire and Daniel seem slightly on edge.

"I can't make you believe in monsters," Scott says. "But I can damn sure make you believe in me."

Scott looks at Daniel. "Now kill that fucking whore, Danny Boy. Quit being a retard."

Daniel nervously stares at Scott.

"Do it now, Danny!" Scott yells.

"You called me a retard," Daniel mumbles.

"I was just fucking around, Daniel. Now do it. Kill that fucking bitch."

Daniel looks down at Elise, determined, but hesitant.

"Do it, dammit," Scott says. "Don't act so fucking stupid."

"I'm not stupid," Daniel says.

"Then fucking kill that bitch, you fucking retard!"

Daniel snaps, "I'm not a retard!" he thrusts his arm out, aiming his gun at Scott, but Scott fires his gun first, hitting Daniel in the chest.

Claire screams and runs for Daniel. She grabs the gun and points it at Scott.

"What the fuck is wrong with you!" She screams at Scott.

"He was gonna shoot me," Scott says. "It was just a reaction, Claire. I couldn't stop it."

Daniel moans in Claire's arms. "Daniel," she says frantically. "Are you okay? You're gonna be okay. We're gonna get you some help."

Claire looks at Scott again. "We have to get him out of here. We have to get him to a doctor."

Scott watches as Claire moves Daniel back to his chair. "That's impossible, Claire. The storm is getting worse out there. We can't go anywhere."

"This is so fucked up," Claire says. "This is not how this shit was supposed to go. I want to leave, now!"

"We can leave when we are done here," Scott says.

"We don't have time, Scott. My brother is

gonna fucking die if we don't get out of here now!"

"Do you want the fucking money or not!" Scott snaps. He stares at Claire. Claire stares back. Daniel breathes heavy.

"It's okay," Daniel says. "It was an accident. We can wait. I want the money, Claire."

Finally, Claire lowers her gun. Everyone is silent for a moment. Taylor, staring at her brother's bleeding corpse on the floor, rage building inside of her, rushes at Scott. "I'm going to kill you for what you've done."

Scott snickers and rolls his eyes. "Sweetie, I am just getting started." He punches her in the face, and catches her as she falls.

"Watch the others," he says to Claire. "I'll be right back."

Claire, cradling her wounded brother, grins as she watches Scott carry Taylor down the hall, into the bathroom.

Inside the bathroom, Scott drops Taylor to the floor. She moans and squirms in pain as he closes the door. He kneels down on the floor beside her, and picks her up, cradles her in his arms.

"There, there, sweetheart. Tell daddy what's the matter."

Taylor stretches her neck and bites into

Scott's cheek, pulling away a chunk of bloody flesh.

"You little fucking bitch!"

Scott turns her over, shoving her head into the toilet bowl, holding her down, her face submerged in the dirty water, as he spanks her ass.

"You're just gonna have to learn to show some manners to adults when they are in your presence, little girl!"

Taylor tries to scream, but instead her mouth and throat fill with water, and then her lungs. Her muscles tense and jerk, she fights hard to break free. But it is no use. In little time at all, her body goes limp, and Scott allows her body to collapse to the bathroom floor.

Scott sits down beside her body, stroking her back gently with his hand. He feels exhausted. He is trying to catch his breath, but he needs a few minutes.

"I'm sorry, sweetheart," he says to the teenager's corpse. "Shit got a little bit crazy out there. But look at you. You are so beautiful. So sweet. So dark and brooding. So soft. How could I not kill you. But, look at it this way. I did you a favor. There was no way you were leaving this house alive. If you had lived any longer, your death would have been much, much worse. I needed to kill something. I needed to quench that thirst. I killed your brother out of reflex. I killed you out of desire. And I let you have it easy. And I'm going to leave you intact. I want to fuck your precious body. I want to thrust inside that tight little corpse cunt. I just want to bury my cock in your lower intestines. You see, I love to fuck dead bodies. I fucking love it. But I'm trying not to get too carried away right now. I've got my eye on your brother's whore girlfriend out there. I think I'm gonna fuck her corpse. What's that..? Oh, she's not dead? No. Not yet. But she will be. And it's gonna be bad. I'm not gonna let her have it easy. I promise. You might want to keep your eyes closed."

Scott reaches over and closes Taylor's eyelids with his fingertips.

"Sweet dreams are made of these," he whispers as he kisses her cheek. He stares at a label marked TOILET, stuck to the porcelain tank. After a quiet moment, he stands up and heads back out into the living room.

"Did you fuck her," Claire asks as Scott walks up.

"No. I wasn't in the mood."

Daniel is sitting in the chair, moaning, sobbing.

"Is he still crying?" Scott asks.

"Don't be an asshole," Claire says. "He really needs help."

"Fuck that," Scott says. "He just needs some

cheering up."

He walks over to the stack of comic books on a table in the corner. He grabs a couple and walks them over to Daniel.

"I'm real sorry, Danny Boy. I didn't mean for this to happen. I'm gonna get you some help, but we can't leave right now. We gotta finish up some business here first. And besides, the weather is just too shitty out there. I doubt we'd even make to a doctor. They probably left town like everybody else. We're all alone out here. So these funny books are just a little something to help you pass the time."

"Those are mine," Frankie says, nervously.

"Shut it, Nerdo, don't get me started with you," Scott says, casting Frankie a hateful glance. "These are Daniel's now. He's worked real hard, and he deserves a treat."

Daniel takes the comic books in his bloody hands. He flips through them, finally settling on an issue of *Power Girl*, a DC Comics superwoman-like character famous for her trademark massive bust line.

"She's got some big titties, don't she Scott?"

"Yes, she does buddy."

Daniel grins, and begins to fondle himself through his pants.

"See there," Scott says to Claire. "He's feeling better already. Everything is going to work out just fine."

Everyone's attention is pulled away to the sudden sound of knocking on the front door. Scott and Claire look at each other with surprise, quietly wondering why they had not noticed the blue strobe lights flashing in the window until this moment.

And that was "Rain King" by Sonic Youth. I always loved those guys. Got a local update for you guys. As I understand it, local police are making last minute runs throughout the area. This is strictly volunteer on their part. God bless them, getting out in this wind and rain, just to check up on us idiots who were stupid enough to stay home during the hurricane. So if you get a cop at your door, invite them in, give them some coffee, let them know you appreciate their concern. This is when they are the good guys, you know. They're not hiding in the bushes waiting to give you a speeding ticket or catch that busted tail light. They are trying to serve and protect right now. And I applaud each and every one of you outstanding officers who are out there tonight trying to help. But I gotta say, you might be as dumb as the rest of us. I mean that in the kindest way possible (laughs). Let's play some Ozzy for the boys in blue out there. This is "Black Rain" on KMRG, your Mighty Rock Gods, 99.9 FM.

"What the *fuck*, Scott?"

Claire watches Scott for some sign that he is still in control of things. The last several minutes have proven to her that he is not as organized as she originally suspected. But now, with those blue lights flashing outside, she needs him to be the mother fucking lizard king.

Everyone else is hoping against hope that this is the safe moment they have been waiting for. The police are here. Certainly this nightmare of a night will be soon at an end.

"Scott?" Claire says.

Scott says nothing. He just closes his eyes. There is another round of knocking on the front door. After a little hesitation, Scott opens his eyes and says "They come to snuff the rooster," and goes to answer the door.

There are two cops, a male and female, standing on the small porch. Scott eyes them warily. They simply stare back. Suspiciously, Scott believes.

"Can I help you, officers?"

"Yes sir," the male cop, his name tag reads Laugier, says. "We are just making our final rounds of the area. We want to make sure everything is all right for any of you who are not evacuating."

"We are letting the residents know that there is still time to get out of the area," the female cop, her tag reads Aja, says. "The whole area is on lockdown, but we have been allowing people to leave for about an hour or so now."

"This is our last stop before we lock ourselves in back at the station," Officer Laugier adds.

"That's great," Scott says. "I think we are holding up just fine here."

"And how many people are here in this house," Officer Laugier asks.

"About ten," Scott says.

"Hurricane party?" Officer Aja asks, with a grin.

"Oh it's a hell of a party," Scott says with a wink. "Would you two like to come in for a few minutes?"

"We're on duty," Officer Laugier says. "But

I appreciate the offer. If all is good here, we'll check you off our list and be on our way."

"All is good," Scott says.

Behind him, in the house, Elise squeals "Don't leave!" Claire rushes at her, putting her gun against her head, threatening to shoot her if she doesn't shut the hell up.

"What was that noise," Officer Laugier asks, attempting to peer over Scott's shoulder into the house.

"That was," Scott starts, then falters. "Um, that was my cat, I think."

"You know," Officer Laugier says, his thin moustache twitching a little, "I think we will come inside for a moment."

"Of course," Scott says, opening the door a little wider. The cops step inside, and they look at the group of people sitting on the living room floor. They barely register the blood on the floor, they just glimpse Gary's body, Daniel bleeding in a chair off to the side, the sound of the door gently closing behind them. Scott is quick. His gun is raised, aimed at the back of Officer Aja's blonde-haired head.

"Keep your fucking hands where I can see them," Scott says. The cops raise their hands, and Claire quickly relieves them of their weapons.

"Get their cuffs," Scott says. "Cuff them together."

Claire forces the cops to stand back-to-back, and puts the handcuffs on them, interlacing the chains of the cuffs.

"You're making a terrible mistake," Officer Laugier says.

"That seems to be the running theme tonight," Scott says, smiling wide.

"Hey Scott. You caught yourself a beast with two bellies," Daniel says, laughing.

"That was a good one, Danny Boy."

Daniel smiles with pride. The bullet wound hurts so much, but it's starting to feel a little better. Getting a little more numb. And he likes that. He was scared he wouldn't be able to enjoy the rest of the night. But now, now he's watching his sister retrieving a knife from the kitchen. She cuts at the cop's uniforms. Tearing the clothing away in strips. Until they are completely naked, their bare flesh streaked with little cuts where the knife cut a little too deep.

"Get on the fucking floor," Scott says to Officer Laugier. "On your fucking belly."

Sweating, Officer Laugier does as he is told. He lies down on the floor, on his stomach, so that Officer Aja is on her back, exposed to the room in all her sexy, authoritative glory.

"Hey pig," Scott says to her as he kneels down beside her. "Yeah, you, pig."

"Please don't hurt us," Officer Aja says.

"Don't be like that," Scott says, rubbing her left thigh. "I'm sure you know how these things go. If you cooperate, it goes much smoother. If you get difficult, well, then everything else gets difficult."

Scott grabs her vagina. She lets out an irritated moan. Scott kisses her breasts, begins fingering her.

"What's inside a girl?" Scott asks. "Ain't no harder question in the so-called civilized world. Oh, give me a peek."

"Leave her alone," Officer Laugier says from underneath her.

"Mind your own business," Scott says. "Me and Miss Piggy here are trying to get acquainted."

Scott begins to finger her harder. He bites her nipple. Bites her breast. Hard. Drawing blood.

"Oh god, please stop," Officer Aja says. "You don't have to do this."

"Bitch, you got it all wrong," Scott says, unzipping his pants and climbing on top of her. "There is so much I have to do. I just can't seem to help myself."

Scott rams his cock deep inside of her. Officer Aja chokes on a scream, instead releasing a low groan.

"Oh baby, don't you know I suffer," Scott says into her ear. "Oh baby, can you hear me moan."

"Please stop," Officer Aja begs. "Please."

"Goddamn it," Scott says. He punches her in the face. Then again. Three times, breaking her nose. Scott spits in her face. "You really need to loosen up, sweetheart."

"I swear to god," Officer Laugier says. "I am gonna seriously fuck you up, son."

"Them sounds like fightin' woids, dad," Scott says, chuckling. He begins punching Officer Aja in her stomach, in between thrusts of his cock.

Finally, it is all too much to take. Officer Aja's bowels give out, and she shits all over herself. Some of the shit gets on Scott and Officer Laugier.

"You nasty fucking bitch," Scott says laughing. "Look at this mess you've made. You should know better, young lady. We are guests in John's lovely house. This is just unacceptable."

Scott scrapes a handful of the shit off the male cop and crams it into Officer Aja's reluctant mouth, smearing brown streaks across her cheek and chin.

"Eat up, sweetheart," he says. "If you can make this mess, you can help clean it up."

She gags, tries to spit it out, tries to scream, but Scott clamps her mouth shut with his hands.

"Eat your mess, cunt! Chew it up and swallow! It's good for you!" Officer Aja struggles more. Scott grips her nose with his other hand, preventing her from breathing. "I said swallow, you fucking cunt!"

Finally, involuntarily, she swallows, the spongy, pungent feces warm as it slides down her throat. Scott takes his hands away.

"Good girl. Now, was that so bad?"

As if in response, Officer Aja tenses up, and vomits the shit from her stomach, along with blood and whatever else she had to eat earlier.

"Oh for Christ's sake," Scott says, rolling his eyes. "You are such a fucking pussy."

Scott takes the knife and starts to gently rub it across her body. The knife causes goosebumps to spring up all over Officer Aja's body, but it is not because of any sort of excited pleasure.

"Please, I have kids," Officer Aja says. "I'm a single mother. I am all they've got."

"Well, I'm afraid your kids are gonna have to make due with a little less," Scott says and he begins to stab her to death. Each stab of the knife becoming more aggressive than the last, bits of flesh peel away, chips of bone flung into the air, blood flowing like a crimson fountain.

"You fucking son of a bitch," Officer Laugier screams. "I'm gonna fucking kill you!"

Hot blood runs down onto him. Covers him.

"Don't be such a dipshit, man," Scott says. "You know you've been thinking about that sexy pussy of hers. Can you smell it? That fresh fucked cunt?"

Scott shoves his fingers into her dead pussy and forces them into Officer Laugier's mouth.

"Taste that? Sweet, ain't it? You play your cards right, maybe I'll let you fuck her dead pussy before I gut you."

"YOU FUCKING COCKSUCKING FAGGOT MOTHER FUCKER, I'M GONNA FUCK YOU UP, YOU FUCK. YOU ARE SO FUCKING FUCKED!"

"He's a feisty one," Claire says.

"You want to play with him?" Scott asks.

Claire smiles and walks over, pushing the cops over with her foot so that Officer Laugier is now facing up.

"Looks like he's already got a little chubby," Claire says, laughing.

She does a sort of lap dance over the cop. Moving her hips from side to side, teasing the head of his dick with her crotch, before finally reaching down to grab it.

"You know, my uncle, my mom's brother, he was a cop. When I was eleven years old he taught me how to shoot a gun, a Smith & Wesson .38 Special. Heavy motherfucker. He made a target out of cardboard, set it out about twenty feet, and I tore that shit up. He was really fucking impressed. Told me that my grouping was fucking exceptional. He asked me how it felt, shooting the gun. I told him I liked it. I fucking loved it. He said he liked watching me shoot. Said I looked sexy. So I shot it some more, and you know what? He started playing with himself. So I took off my shirt, and shot some more. And then he started to jerk himself off. So I took off my pants. And then the rest. And I kept shooting. Then I went over and grabbed his huge dick and just started sucking and sucking. I let him fuck my face so hard, it made my asshole scream. Oh fucking Jesus, how he moaned. 'Oh Claire, you are so sweet. You are so precious. I love you so much.' And so I fucked him. He said my pussy was the best he'd ever had. And we fucked all the time after that. Still do, like at family reunions and shit. So, I got a thing for cops, you know. It's the uniform, I think. That shiny fucking badge just makes me so fucking wet. Too bad your uniform is in a hundred little pieces... Oh wait!"

Claire goes over to the pile of destroyed police uniforms.

"Here we go," she says, pulling out a strip of blue shirt with a badge attached and brings it over.

"Oh shit, I think this is your partner's badge," she says. "Well, I guess it's good enough."

She opens the pin on the back of the silver badge and pushes it into the thick flesh of Officer Laugier's chest, right above his heart. The cop screams in pain.

"Shut your whining," she says. "Momma's gonna make all of your nightmares come true. Momma's gonna put all of her fears into you."

"Nice one, sweetie," Scott says.

Claire winks at him, then gets down on her knees and begins to suck on the cop's dick. He cries in protest, but still moans a little.

"Being a cop is dangerous, kiddies," Scott says to the group of captives. "But it sure has it's perks, huh?"

He watches Claire suck the dick. She fondles Officer Laugier's balls with one hand, and with her other slips a finger deep into his anus. The cop twitches around, begging for her to stop.

"Fuck this shit," Scott says.

He pulls Claire away, and uncuffs the cop. He rolls the female cop bloody corpse over, and puts a gun to Officer Laugier's head.

"Now you're gonna fuck your partner," Scott says.

Officer Laugier begins crying.

"God dammit, be a fucking man and get to it!" Scott pushes him down on top of the corpse. "Now fuck that nasty fucking dead ass pussy or I'm gonna splatter your head all over this fucking place!"

Officer Laugier does as he is told. He slips his dick into the corpse and begins to thrust, in and out, in and out. He begins to choke a little, and vomits on the corpse.

"This is so fucking hot," Claire says.

She goes over and fondles his balls. After a few minutes, she feels his balls begin to tighten.

"Pull out, mother fucker!" She says, pulling his hips back and he spews cum all over Officer Aja's corrupted body.

Claire laughs and grabs Officer Laugier in a big hug from behind.

"Wanna know a secret?" Claire whispers

into his ear. "I've got a Little Satan that lives in my belly, and he tells me things. He tells me what to do. Do you want to know what he's telling me right now? I'll give you a hint: You're going to scream."

Claire takes a gun and shoves the barrel up the cop's asshole and pulls the trigger. A hot blast explodes from the gun, erupting into his rectum. Officer Laugier's body spasms wildly as he screams out in sheer horror.

Claire drops the gun to the floor and grabs her knife. She arches her back, spreading her arms up into the air above her. She closes her eyes and proclaims, with absolute passion:

> *O you, most cunning and beautiful of all*
> *angels,*
> *Betrayed by God, and by fate, deprived of*
> *praise,*
> *O Satan, take pity of my long misery!*

Claire then reaches around with the knife and slits the cop's throat open. Blood pours out to cover the cum and sweat and vomit Officer Aja's female corpse. Officer Laugier slumps over on top of her, and Claire and Scott start dancing around like wild Indians, circling the two dead cops. They wipe some of the cop blood on their cheekbones like war paint. And they begin to sing, in abysmal harmony: "Doesn't it make you feel better, the pigs have won tonight, and they can all sleep soundly, 'cause everything is all right."

They make loud whoop-whoop-whoop

Indian sounds, clapping the palms of their hands against their mouths. Finally, Claire and Scott collapse into each other's arms, laughing, crying out of their uncontrollable joy.

"Claire," Daniel says. "You still fuck Uncle Greg?"

Claire looks at her brother. "Fuck no. I haven't seen that pervert in ten years."

She laughs frenziedly.

"Okay," Scott says. "I'm done fucking around. Let's get down to business."

He looks around at the captives. He points his gun at John.

"You, kemosabe. I'm going to need some fucking rope."

*Yeah. We've got reports of several deaths already.
I'm sure there is more to come. This is the part I
hate the most, you know. The storm is in really high
gear. I'm hoping the station can take it. She's been
through this all before, so we should be fine. I hope
everyone boarded their windows up. And chained
their cars to the ground for that matter (laughs).
The phone lines are down, but one of the last
requests we got a few hours ago from a guy named
Kenny. This one's for you, Kenny. Black Label
Society. "Downpour," on KMRG 99.9 FM.*

John is forced at gunpoint to tie his friends onto chairs, which are placed in a circle. Even Gary's body is tied to a chair.

In a kitchen drawer, Scott has found John's little green plastic label-maker. Turning the white dial on top to choose the desired letters, then squeezing the trigger to force the letters onto a strip of black, adhesive-backed plastic, Scott makes a personalized label for everyone.

"We are going to play musical chairs," Scott says. "But my rules are a little different."

He walks over to take the knife away from Claire and he begins to walk clockwise around the circle of chairs. Starting at Frankie, he sticks a label with the word FAGGOT to his forehead.

"When the music is playing," he says "I will be walking. Circling you, like a vulture."

At Elise, he applies a label marked CUNT.

"But when the music stops, I will stop."

On Gary's dead forehead, a label marked HERO.

"And then I will cut the throat of whoever I am standing behind. Sound like fun?"

On Wesley's forehead, a label marked PUSSY. On Maggie's forehead, a label marked WHOA BLACK BETTY. And finally, for John, a label marked simply with the word KING.

"I really like your castle," Scott says to John with a wink and a malevolent smile.

Claire turns on the radio, and Scott begins to walk slowly around the captives. When he gets behind Frankie, Claire stops the music.

"Sorry, Nerdo," Scott says. He reaches around and runs the knife across Frankie's throat. Blood flows out wild, the others scream, helpless in their binds.

Except for Elise. Somehow, she manages to slip out of her ropes. She jumps up and runs off. She is out the door before Scott realizes what has happened, but he quickly heads after her.

The rain is pouring outside, and the wind is terribly violent. They are in the middle of the worst part of the hurricane.

Scott catches up with Elise and knocks her to the ground. He climbs on top of her, staring into her eyes. He smiles.

"Your pretty face is going to hell," he says.

Scott begins to punch Elise in the head and face, over and over, breaking her nose, busting her lower lip, blackening her eyes, breaking her left cheekbone. Eventually, he quits. He takes a deep breath. He looks down at her, with some sort of twisted pity in his eyes.

"When I was ten years old, I killed my brother. He was seven. He had dug in my toy box without permission and accidentally broke the left arm off my favorite toy. A Ninja Turtle. Michaelangelo. The one with the orange mask and the nunchucks. I was so pissed off. I choked him to death, right there in our room. My parents didn't notice for nearly five hours. They sent me to a psychiatric hospital for a few years. When I was thirteen I raped the twelve year old daughter of one of my doctors. She had come to visit him at the hospital. I said I would show her around. I pushed her into a bathroom and fucked her on the floor. I got into a lot of trouble. I was so stupid back then. In hindsight, I know I made a big mistake that day. I know now, I should have killed her. I should have smashed her little face into the floor, over and over until there was nothing left but pulpy meat and bones and blood."

Scott stretches back, tilts his head up. The cold water just falls all over him. For a moment, he is completely lost in tranquility. Not a care in the world.

Elise just stares up at him, sobbing and trembling, behind dark, swollen eyes.

"Come on," he finally says, standing up and stretching his arms with a groan. "Let's get you back inside before you catch a cold."

Scott heads back towards the house, dragging Elise behind him.

..and I don't know how much longer things can hold up here at the station. It's bad out there. Really fucking bad. Shit! Sorry about that. Guess we'll have a little FCC fine waiting for us when this is all over.. What? I did? Twice? Damn it. It's so loud, the rain and wind is just pounding the walls of the station. I'm starting to think this wasn't such a hot idea. What about you Trey? Yeah. Sage has been hiding in the bathroom for the last hour or so (loud crashing sound) What the hell was that? .. I don't know either. It could have been the satellite dish or someth--SYSTEM ALERT. SYSTEM ALERT. SYSTEM ALERT. KMRG SIGNAL COMPROMISED. WEATHER ALERT. STRONG WINDS. HEAVY RAIN. STAY INSIDE. DO NOT LEAVE YOUR HOMES. SYSTEM ALERT. SYSTEM ALERT. SYSTEM ALERT. KMRG SIGNAL COMPROMISED. WEATHER ALERT. STRONG WINDS. HEAVY RAIN. STAY INSIDE. DO NOT LEAVE YOUR HOMES. SYSTEM ALERT. SYSTEM ALERT. SYSTEM ALERT. KMRG SIGNAL COMPROMISED. WEATHER ALERT. STRONG WINDS. HEAVY RAIN. STAY INSIDE. DO NOT LEAVE YOUR HOMES. SYSTEM ALERT. SYSTEM ALERT. SYSTEM ALERT. KMRG SIGNAL

COMPROMISED. WEATHER ALERT. STRONG WINDS. HEAVY RAIN. STAY INSIDE. DO NOT LEAVE YOUR HOMES. SYSTEM ALERT. SYSTEM ALERT. SYSTEM ALERT. KMRG SIGNAL COMPROMISED--(white noise. dead air)

Back inside the house, Scott sits Elise back into her chair. He does not bother tying her down. He knows that she is too weak to fight back at all.

He begins to rub her breasts with his hands. Massaging them, stroking the nipples. He grips her left breast in his hand, giving it a firm squeeze. He leans in close to her ear.

"Mother," he says. "Tell your children not to hear my words."

He takes his knife and slices off her left breast. Elise is barely conscious, but still moans in obvious pain and distress. Scott leaves her sitting there, crying and bleeding, and goes into the kitchen. He had noticed the food processor earlier, it still has some margarita mix in it, and he drops in the handful of breast-meat. He hits the large white button, blending the meat down to a fatty, bloody pulpy mess.

He stares at the concoction for a moment. He takes a glass, and pours in the bloody mush. He takes the glass back into the living room, and extends it to Elise.

"Drink up, doll."

Elise looks up briefly at the glass, then turns away.

"Come on, sweetheart," Scott says. "It's good for you. All natural."

He pushes the glass against her mouth. She tightens her lips shut.

"Don't fight it, babe."

Elise moves her head from side to side, trying to avoid contact with the glass. Frustrated, Scott shoves his knife against her throat.

"Drink your fucking titty juice, you fucking cunt! Do it or I'm gonna cut your throat and let you bleed the fuck out!"

Elise opens her mouth to groan, and Scott thrusts the rim of the glass into the gaping aperture. Elise can not fight it, and the warm, salty mixture flows into her mouth and down her throat. She gags and coughs. She vomits the mess back up.

"There now," Scott says. "Why can't bitches just drink what they're given? Why do you all have to put up such a fucking fight?"

"Please.." Elise begins to say.

"No," Scott interrupts. "We don't have time for that shit right now."

He reaches high into the air with his knife. "Let's go, baby," he says. "I am the mad mad daddy!" He thrusts down, stabbing her in her head. The knife plunges in and out several times. Scott can feel, with each stab, the dense bone of Elise's skull chipping away and eventually giving way to the wet, soft brain matter no longer protected within. Elise wants to scream, to fight for her life, but she is paralyzed. Her eyes bulge in shock and disbelief. White flashes of light explode in her mind's eye with every intrusion of the metal blade into her head. After the tenth or twelfth stab, could be more as it is hard to keep track after so many, her eyes roll back. Her body, moments ago locked in tense muscular petrifaction, goes limp, blood running from her mouth and nose and ears and eyes and the multiple wounds in the top of her head.

Scott kicks her body to the floor. Elise's corpse lands on it's left side and Scott drops to his knees. He rubs his hands all over her head, wetting the palms with her hot fresh blood. He then uses the blood to lubricate her asshole, tapping at the tiny rear hole with his middle finger. Elise is quite dead, but for a brief moment Scott believes he feels her asshole pucker out of anticipation. His cock swells, getting bigger and harder than he has ever felt before. He thrusts a finger into the hole, then two fingers, greasing the inside with the warm blood.

"You say goodbye," Scott says as he unzips his pants. "And I say hello."

He climbs on top of Elise's corpse and thrusts his cock into her blood-lubed back door. He pounds and pounds, wailing and squealing with lustful delight. He seizes at her dead flesh with harsh grips. He bites into her shoulder. He rubs his feet against her bloody legs. He smells her hair, scented with sweat, mud and blood.

John steals a glance at his friends. Wesley is just staring off into an empty corner. He seems to be whispering to himself. Praying, perhaps. Wesley's family was religious, but he had not attended church he was a kid. *Old habits*, John thinks to himself. Then, other thoughts. *I should not have invited them here,* his mind screams. *This is all my fault. And there is nothing I can do.* His stomach churns, bubbling with bile and hopelessness. Tears fill his eyes as he turns his attention to Maggie.

Maggie is staring at John. Watching him cry. Her eyes, though swollen with tears as well, seem to be speaking to him. *It's okay, John. We're going to be okay.*

John just stares back. Her eyes are all that he can see. Her beautiful, glorious, exquisitely heavenly eyes. But it's a small comfort. It's the sound that is pushing him over the brink. The sound of Scott, his cock thrashing in and out, the bloody suction-cup pop of Elise's anus as the swollen sex goes in and out. In and out. Pop.

In and out. Pop. In and out. Pop.

"You are fantastic," Scott whispers into Elise's dead ear. "Better than I expected. Better than I even dreamed."

Scott abruptly pulls his cock out of the bloody hole. He slides himself up, so that his crotch is closer to Elise's head. Using his right index finger and thumb, he plunges into Elise's left eye, and rips the eye out of the socket. He shoves the head of his cock into the vacant socket, and begins to stroke himself. When he cums, the milky discharge fills the socket, overflowing out and running down the side of Elise's face.

"Cum goes in the eye socket," Scott says, picking the wet eyeball from the floor while parting Elise's dead thighs. "And the eye goes in the cum socket."

He crams the eyeball into the alcove of the dead vagina. He pulls the legs apart for everyone to see. The eyeball was positioned perfectly, so that it appears to be peeking out of the fleshy orifice.

"Ever get the feeling that you are being watched?!" Scott exclaims with a boastful laugh.

Finally, Scott's laughter dies down. He composes himself, and stands up. He kicks the desecrated corpse.

"Damn," he says. "This bitch really had it coming huh?"

Scott walks over and grabs John by the back

of the neck. "That was all your fault, you know. You didn't tie her up very well!"

"I ran out of rope," John says, shaking.

"Well," Scott says. "I need to teach you a lesson."

He puts the knife in John's hand. "It's your turn to play."

At gunpoint, John starts to walk around his friends, the music blaring loud. When he gets behind Wesley, Claire stops the music. John freezes.

"Go ahead, John," Scott says. "This is where you show us all how much of a man you are."

John tries to stall, but he can not fight this.

"I'm sorry, Wesley," he says, and then cuts his friend's throat open wide.

Maggie screams as blood sprays out in an arc from Wesley's throat. John drops the knife to the floor and takes Maggie in his arms, telling her that he's sorry. So very sorry. They cry together.

"Ain't this some romantic-ass bullshit," Scott says.

Daniel, who has been in a chair off to the side, begins coughing up blood. Claire goes to him, but it is too late. His body convulses for a moment, then he goes limp. Blood trickling down from the corner of his mouth.

Claire's face grows red with rage. She stands up slowly. She looks at Scott.

"I'm sorry, babe," Scott says. He can see that things are about to get complicated.

"Don't you fucking *babe* me, Scott."

"I don't know what to say."

"This took too long," Claire barks. "We could have gotten him help!"

"There was no time, Claire! Look, this is not the time to start getting goofy on me!"

"You are a crazy fucking piece of shit. You are a fucking asshole, Scott!"

"What the hell was I supposed to do, Claire?!"

The yelling between Scott and Claire grows more intense, and does not show any sign of letting up soon.

Maggie leans closer to John to whisper. "I love you. I have always loved you. I don't want to die without telling you."

John is overwhelmed with emotion. He looks into her eyes with a brave new determination.

"We're not going to die, Maggie."

Slowly, he picks up the knife from the floor, and cuts her rope. "We've got this one chance," he says. "We're gonna have to run. Okay?"

Maggie nods. "I love you."

"I love you, too."

John and Maggie take off running, heading for the door, hidden by the heat of their captors' argument. John trips and stumbles just as Maggie nears the door. Distracted by the fall, Scott turns and fires his gun, hitting Maggie in the back. With a scream she stumbles out the door, disappearing into the rainy darkness.

"NO!" John shrieks, getting to his feet, and flinging himself out the door. John falls to the ground, lifting Maggie's head, cradling her in his arms.

"Maggie don't leave me," he begs. "Don't you leave me here."

Maggie starts to speak, but instead she spits up a mouthful of blood. Her nerves are twitching all over her body.

"It's okay, Maggie," he says. "You're gonna be fine. Just hold on."

She gives him a fleeting smile, and with a bloody gargled exhale, her body goes limp.

"No!" John screams. "Maggie! No, Maggie! Just hold on, baby! Please don't go. Please don't go. Please wake up. Please. Please, I love you. I'm sorry. I'm so sorry.."

John holds Maggie's body to his chest, squeezing her. Shaking. Hoping she will wake up. But she won't. She never will.

Scott is standing in the doorway, looking down at John and Maggie. Scott feels a sort of nervous twitch in his left eye. Something he realizes he hasn't felt in a very long time. Behind him, he hears the click of a pistol being cocked. He turns around, and sees Claire standing in the center of the room, with her gun pointed at him.

"You just manage to fuck everything up, don't you?" Claire says.

"Things got out of hand, Claire."

She just stares at him. "Drop your gun," she says.

Scott drops his gun.

"I love you," she says.

"I love you, too."

Claire gets a more anguished look on her face. "I loved Daniel more."

Scott sighs to himself. He calms his nerves. He stares intently at Claire. At her gun.

"For those about to rock," Scott begins, but he is interrupted by Claire.

She says "Fire," and pulls the trigger on her gun. The bullet explodes from the barrel, hitting Scott in the left eye, pulverizing the brain as the bullet slips through the back of his skull and disappears into the stormy darkness outside. Scott's body collapses to the floor. Claire just stands there, arms outstretched, finger still tight on the squeezed trigger, and she begins to sob quietly.

John comes through the door. He looks down at Scott's motionless body. Then, he looks at Claire, still sobbing to herself.

"I'm sorry about all of this," Claire says. John just stares at her.

"I really am," she says, closing her eyes.

John watches her nervously fidget with the gun in her hand. He's not sure what to do. Should he run? Should he try to attack her? Get the gun away? He feels so numb, he wonders if death would not be such a bad thing right now. Then, before he can come to a decision himself, Claire unveils a plan of her own. She puts the gun against the side of her own head and fires. Bits of skull and blood and brain matter cloud the air as her body drops to the floor. John stands there, silently among the bodies and blood, as the howling hurricane blows outside.

He is in absolute total shock. The numbness is overwhelming. There is so much blood. So much silence. He is alone. He is alive. But he is all alone.

Finally, John walks back out the door. The rain has passed, but the wind is still strong, and it nearly knocks him over as he steps around Maggie's body. He tries hard not to look down at her. Part of him thinks if he does, he might see that she is alive. Part of him thinks that she might try to attack him. Some undead thing. The events of the night, and all of the alcohol and drugs, are messing with his mind. He glances down at her anyway. She is stagnant. She is dead. He keeps moving. He concentrates his sights on the police squad car sitting off to his right. He blocks out thoughts of the torture and murder of the cops. He just walks, faster now.

He makes it to the car, opens the passenger door, and sits down on the cool seat. His muscles relax. He lets his breathing ease up a little. Then he reaches for the two-way radio.

"Hello?" he asks. "Is there anybody in there?"

He waits, silently. There is only static for a few moments.

"Just nod if you can hear me."

"This is dispatch," a female voice suddenly crackles over the radio. "Go ahead."

"I need help."

"Who am I speaking with?" the woman says. "What is the problem, sir?"

"I need to report a murder," John says, his voice catching in his throat for a moment. "Several murders."

"Can you give me your name, sir? And your location?"

John leans his head back. His thoughts are racing. His stomach acid is churning.

"Are you there, sir? Are you all right?"

John closes his eyes. He can feel the bile bubbling in the back of his throat. He tries to clear his head. But he can't. His mind has drifted back to a very particular dinner meeting he had just over a month ago.

The atmosphere inside Harlequin's Steakhouse is one of laid back sophistication, with that ever-present southern vibe that is found in every other restaurant in Lake Charles, Louisiana. John is sitting at a table near the fireplace in the main dining hall. He has ordered the pork chop dinner, a huge two-inch thick cut of meat grilled to perfection on the bone. He specified the meat well done, since he really does not trust undercooked pork. The waiter, a short stocky guy dressed in white shirt and black vest, his name given as Jarrett, has just refilled John's glass of sweet tea and informed him that his food should be out shortly. John took the liberty of ordering a steak, medium, for his dinner guest, whom he is still waiting for.

John glances around the dining room. There are other guests having dinner, but not so many that it should compromise this important meeting tonight. John is dressed in black slacks and a red button-down dress shirt. His hair is combed back, neat. He hasn't shaved in over a month and has a decent beard. Even his dead parents wouldn't recognize him right now. He takes a drink from his sweet tea, removing the wedge of lemon from the rim and setting it aside. Someone cautiously approaches John on his right.

"John?"

John looks up to greet the man, who is wearing a grey dress shirt and black tie, with black slacks. His long black hair is parted on the side and pulled back in a tight ponytail. "I hope I'm not overdressed. You said this place has a dress code."

"That's fine," John says. "Have a seat."

The man sits down, opposite of John. The waiter momentarily arrives to request a drink order. The man orders a beer. Coors light.

"So," the man begins. "Should we get down to business, or what?"

"Well," John says, clearing his throat. "We've discussed the basic details by email. I just want to make sure that you are serious. That you can handle what I am proposing."

"For the money you're offering, I've got no problem doing anything to help you out with your situation. The question is, can *you* handle this?"

"I am totally resigned to what I have planned."

"But these guys, the ones you'll have at your house, they're your friends, right?"

"My best friends."

"Just makes this kinda fucked up, you know."

"That's the point."

"Just so I have this straight," the man pauses as his beer, along with both orders of food, arrives. They thank the waiter, who nods and leaves. "I want to be sure of what's going on. You are inviting your best friends to your house, so that me and my, shall we say associates, can come in, lay waste to everyone, except for you and this one girl."

"Maggie. Yes, that's the plan."

"And all so that you and this Maggie, the sole survivors of this grand massacre, will achieve some deep mystical connection as a result of the shared tragedy."

John nods his head in agreement.

"Look," the man says. "I've done some pretty crazy shit, been a part of some fucked up shit over the years. I'm just saying, I consider myself a pretty bad dude, you know."

"Sure."

"But this, this is just freaky, man. Borderline genius."

"Thanks."

"So I'm good to go, bro. Long as you can pay up."

"I have more than enough money from my parents' inheritance to pay what we agreed. And I'm throwing in another ten grand, because I'm such a nice guy."

"Fair enough. So what's so special about this girl, anyway?"

"Everything," John says. "She's worth risking my sanity over."

"I know it's only rock and roll," the man says. "But I like it."

"What?"

"Nothing," the man says, cutting into his steak and taking a bite. "Goddamn. This is spectacular."

"The best steak in Louisiana," John says, reaching into the bag by his chair to take out a cell phone.

"Here," John says, handing the phone to the man. "This is a prepaid phone. Almost totally untraceable, except when it's actually in use. Do not use this phone except for communicating with me. When I find out when my friends are coming, I'll let you know. I'll text you when they actually arrive at my house. Destroy the phone before you and your

119

associates come."

"Sure," the man says. "No problem. You got this shit all worked out. But what about the weather? You might want to get this all over with before hurricane season kicks in."

"I'll keep that in mind."

John gets up, leaving his food untouched.

"I need to go," John says, setting a handful of twenties on the table. "Enjoy your steak. Take the pork chop with you."

"Thanks," the man says.

John reaches down to shake his hand. "Thank you, Scott. I'll see you in about a month."

John walks out of Harlequin's and makes it to his car just as the bile in his stomach rushes to his throat. John bends over and vomits profusely into the grass bordering the restaurant's parking lot. He wipes his mouth on his sleeve and climbs into his car. In the CD player is the Dax Riggs album *We Sing Of Only Blood Or Love*. The song "Didn't Know Yet What I'd Know When I Was Bleedin'" explodes through the stereo speakers.

John puts the car in gear, heading for Home Depot for more materials before heading home to do more work on the house. His hands are sore from all the work he has put into the house this week.

His next step is to rip up the carpet to expose the hardwood floors underneath. Should make it so much easier when it is time to clean up all the blood.

Good morning everybody. This is Coolhand Madman, here at the KMRG studio, and while we ran into some technical difficulties last night, I'm happy to announce that the station is in one piece. As you are all aware, Hurricane Bataille is out of our area. It turned northeast in the early morning hours, and lost a lot of momentum. It's now a tropical storm, dropping heavy rains on central and northern Mississippi. Our prayers go out to the people there, and to anyone else who has been caught in the storm's path. What I am unhappy to announce is that Bataille did a lot of damage to our area. I am already getting verification of property loss, deaths, missing persons, the terrible aftermath that we are all so used to hearing about after a storm like this. I'm holding my post here until noon today, then someone will come in and take over, so that I can go and check on my own house, which I understand is in pretty good shape, but you never really know until you check it out. I want to thank everyone who called in with news over the night. I hope that as many of you as possible were spared the brunt of the devastation that Hurricane Bataille brought to southwest Louisiana. I have a few calls to make myself, so let's kick off things this morning

with the Rolling Stones, "It's All Over Now," right here on KMRG, your Mighty Rock Gods, 99.9 FM.

Five ambulances full of mutilated bodies. Several police cruisers with detectives asking questions. The crushing smell of blood fresh and strong inside the house. The evidence of Hurricane Bataille's fiendish rampage strong on the outside.

The yard is littered with debris. Tree limbs. Trash cans. Pieces of fence. Pieces of other houses. A dead stray kitten, drowned in a sunken area of the yard. John standing on the porch, speaking with Marianne Sonnier, a female detective. He has told her everything she needs to know.

His friends were visiting for the weekend, when a trio of strangers arrived to rob the house. They took everyone hostage, killing them one by one. Even killing two police officers who stopped to check in. All of the evidence was plain to see. The detective tells John that there will be further investigation, but that he should try to get some rest. The case seems to be pretty cut and dry.

"I'm sorry about your friends," Detective Sonnier says, staring at a little black label marked LOVE that is stuck to a framed photograph of John and Maggie. A photo taken during high school.

"Me too," John says.

The detective is tall and thin. In her mid thirties. Auburn hair. Gorgeous. John catches himself staring at her chest, and looks away nervously.

"If there is anything I can do for you," she says, "anything at all, you call and let me know."

She hands John one of her cards, and smiles as she pats his hand. John grins back to her, slipping the card into his back pocket.

John watches as the detective goes to her car, and waits until the last of the ambulances and patrol cars vanish down the long and winding road away from the house. John goes inside, and locks the door behind him. He goes into his bedroom, his parents' old room, and opens the closet. He finds his father's black bathrobe. He puts it on. Under the kitchen sink, he finds a pair of his mother's yellow rubber gloves. He grabs a mop, and some scrubbing brushes, and begins the long arduous task of cleaning up his mess.

But the old house in the woods of DeQuincy, just northwest of the city of Lake Charles, Louisiana, cannot seem to get properly cleaned. Wearing his father's black bathrobe, with his mother's yellow rubber gloves, John has been mopping and scrubbing and wiping for hours. The progress seems slow. Protracted. Almost futile.

There is so much blood. So much blood.

On the radio, "Keep Yourself Alive" by the seventies rock icons Queen is booming out from local station KMRG 99.9 FM. Maggie's favorite song. John called the station twenty minutes ago to request it. Although the song is rocking and upbeat, tears fill his eyes as he works.

The large house was a real fixer-upper when his parents bought it about two years ago. Inheriting the house after their deaths, John has made it his mission to make this house his home. To make it his own. It really is all that he has left.

In the last couple of weeks he has pretty much finished the main work on the house, and has been dying to show it off. Although now he is beginning to wonder if inviting his friends for the weekend was not a mistake. The place is such a mess. He just can't seem to get it clean. There is so much blood.

So much blood. This had to be a mistake.

John steps out on the small front porch and looks up to the sky. A cool breeze blows through his shaggy, bloodstained, dirty blonde hair. He sees only a few dark clouds. But he knows, this time of year, the rain is never far.

The rain is never far.

THE HURRICANE PARTY
HURRICANE PREPAREDNESS GUIDE

What follows is a collection of extras for you to explore. This is something I did with my second novel, *The Main Course*. Creating DVD-style "extra features" for the reader to indulge in. Technical information about the creation of *The Hurricane Party*, some artwork based on the story, and just whatever else I have decided to throw in. Am I just trying to fill pages, to make my book seem a little bigger than it really is? You bet your sweet ass. But you might as well get something out of it. So here, enjoy some of this shit while I blow some money on comic books and kitchen supplies.

The Saffir-Simpson Hurricane Scale

The Saffir-Simpson Hurricane Scale is a 1-5 rating system based on a given storm's intensity. The scale is used to estimate the destructive power of an oncoming hurricane. Wind speed is the determining factor of the scale, as well as barometric pressure readings in the eye of the hurricane. During normal conditions, the barometric pressure at sea level is about 1,000 millibars. This number drops as a storm forms and intensifies.

Category One Hurricane

Wind speeds of 74-95 mph. A strong, but relatively light storm. Minimal damage, with some flooding, can be expected. Barometric pressure no lower than 980 millibars (mb).

Category Two Hurricane

Wind speeds of 96-110 mph. More flooding can be expected from this considerably more powerful storm. Property damage to homes and trees are common. Barometric pressure at 965 to 979 mb.

Category Three Hurricane

Wind speeds of 111-130 mph. Smaller homes can be destroyed. Land that is lower than 5 feet above sea level can be expected to totally flood at least 8 miles inland of the coast. Barometric pressure at 945 to 964 mb. Evacuation orders for low-lying residences will be issued.

Category Four Hurricane

Wind speeds of 131-155 mph. Storm surge can reach 18 feet above normal. Signs blown down. Trees uprooted. Smaller houses destroyed, with considerable roof damage to larger structures. Land lower than 10 feet above sea level will flood. Barometric pressure at 920 to 944 mb. Massive evacuation orders.

Category Five Hurricane

The motherfucker. Wind speed higher than 165 mph. Complete destruction of small homes, mobile homes, signs and trees. Severe window and door damage. Barometric pressure lower than 920 mb. Massive evacuation of residential areas on low ground within 5-10 miles of coast.

In *The Hurricane Party*, Hurricane Bataille makes landfall as a Category Five storm. The highest wind recordings are at 169 mph, and the barometric pressure at the lowest reading are 913 mb. Hurricane Bataille is a very powerful storm, and causes extensive damage to southeast Louisiana. 138 casualties related to the storm are reported, with hundreds more injured and left homeless.

While Hurricane Bataille is a fictional storm, I am very familiar with the real thing. Hurricanes are one of the deadliest storms created by mother nature.

When a storm poses a threat, especially a Category Three or higher, getting out of the area is a damn good idea. Hurricane parties make for great stories, but in real life you have to deal with power failure, lack of supplies, potential harm and death. A simple power failure in my story would have made things so much worse for my little group of characters, but I am a merciful creator and tried to take it a little easy on them. They had enough to worry about as it was.

THE PERFECT STORM:
The Influences Behind *The Hurricane Party*

The primary influences for the themes I explore in *The Hurricane Party* were the exploitation horror films from the 1970s to the present day. I focused my attention on the films of the French New Wave of horror, a frontrunner in the highly polarizing genre of so-called torture porn, which is provocatively brutal in its violent content, but also dramatically challenging and often dreamlike.

Films such as Alexandre Aja's "Haute Tension," Julien Maury and Alexandre Bustillo's "Inside," Xavier Gens' "Frontier(s)," and Pascal Laugier's "Martyrs" were major influences to me during the writing of this novel. American horror old and new, from "Last House On The Left" and "Deliverance" to "Hostel" and "The Devil's Rejects" were a big part of my diet as well. A lot of these influences were present when I wrote my first book, *The Horns Of Evangelina*, but now I was certainly focusing more on European horror, with an emphasis on these brilliant new French films.

While studying the evolution of the French horror film, I found that the majority of the truly original and shocking breed began in the late 1990s. Before that, fine examples of French *gorenography* are few and far between, the best examples found in the massive filmography of director Jean Rollin, whose work was not exactly an influence on *The Hurricane Party*, but there is a lot of brutal sexuality in his films and I am sure a little of it rubbed off. But the further back I searched, I found that these shocking themes of horror and sexuality leave French cinema completely, and that the roots trace back to literature.

It was in researching the controversial writers of sadistic decadence that I became fascinated with one writer in particular: Georges Bataille.

Georges Bataille was a French writer born in 1897. A highly influential writer, Bataille's work shows a certain obsession for the surreal, with themes centered on human (personal and external) sacrifice, hedonism, and the metaphysical. Incredibly controversial, his writing has been lambasted by critics as nothing more than obscene and sadistic nightmarish erotica.

Bataille's most significant work, his 1928 novella *The Story Of The Eye*, became an obsession of mine while writing *The Hurricane Party*. The sexual depravity and moral ambiguity of his writing just astounded me. Certainly I had read things more vile than this, but never had it been presented so profoundly and intelligently.

I read this novel, as well as other examples of his writing, several times. Bataille's influence on me was so absolute that I named my hurricane in his honor.

Another French writer whose work had an impact on me was Charles Baudelaire (1821-1867). His poems are dark, meticulously crafted, beautifully unholy works of art. One poem in particular, "The Litanies Of Satan" (found in his 1857 collection *Flowers Of Evil*) was so blasphemously poignant that I decided to reference it in *The Hurricane Party*.

Now, I would like to present my own translation of Charles Baudelaire's infamous poem "The Litanies Of Satan," to give you an idea of what makes this man's work of such interest to me.

The Litanies of Satan

O you, most cunning and beautiful of all angels,
Betrayed by God, and by fate, deprived of praise,
O Satan, take pity of my long misery!

O Prince of exile, whom has been wronged
And whom, conquering, shall rise up stronger
O Satan, take pity of my long misery!

You who knows all, great king of subterranean
        things,
Charlatan familiar of human torment,
O Satan, take pity of my long misery!

You who, even with hideousness, with accursed
        odds,
Teaches through love of the sweet flavors of
        Paradise,
O Satan, take pity of my long misery!

O you who through Death, your old and sturdy
          lover,
Generated Hope, - insane folly!
O Satan, take pity of my long misery!

You who make the outlaw's glance calm and proud
Which damns the people around the scaffold.
O Satan, take pity of my long misery!

You who knows in which corners of the earth
A jealous God has hidden precious stones,
O Satan, take pity of my long misery!

You of which the clear eye knows the deep arsenals
Where sleeps buried the people of metals,
O Satan, take pity of my long misery!

You whose broad hands unveil the abyss
With the sleepwalker wandering at the edge of the
          buildings,
O Satan, take pity of my long misery!

You who, with great magic, softened the old bones
Of the sleeping drunkard stomped by the horses,
O Satan, take pity of my long misery!

You who, to comfort the frail men who suffer,
Taught us how to mix nitrate and sulfur,
O Satan, take pity of my long misery!

You who bestows your mark, subtle accessory
Upon the face of pitiless and cheap Crésus,
O Satan, take pity of my long misery!

You who imparts in the eyes and the hearts of
        young girls
The worship of their wound and the love of worldly
        possessions,
O Satan, take pity of my long misery!

Stick of the exiled, lamp of the inventors,
Confessor of the hung and the conspirators,
O Satan, take pity of my long misery!

Adoptive father of those who, with sinister anger,
Drove out God the Father from their earthly
        Paradise,
O Satan, take pity of my long misery!

Prayer

Glory and praise with you,
Satan, in the heights
Sky, where you reigned, and in the depths
Of Hell, where, triumphant, you dream in solace!
Make it so that my heart shall one day, under the
        Tree of Science,
Rest close to you, until the hour invigorates your
        essence,
Like a new Temple its branches will engorge!

- Charles Baudelaire
(Translated from original French by Chuck Morgue)

Obviously another major influence in writing *The Hurricane Party* (as with any other example of my work) is music. I wanted plenty of song references in this novel, and decided that incorporating transcript-style chapters of dialogue from a radio station would be an interesting plot concept. A way of keeping the reader up to date on what Hurricane Bataille is doing, while getting in some of the song references I so greatly desired. Keeping with a theme of weather-related songs proved to be a bit of a challenge, but was very rousing. Trying to have the songs mirror certain moods of the story, when possible, was something I really tried hard to accomplish. I like to think I did okay.

You can get a good idea for the types of music I enjoy by reading this book. Nine Inch Nails, Depeche Mode, The Stooges, Queen, The Doors, Muse, so many of my favorite musical acts get a nod in this book.

The song that John and Wesley perform in the book, "In The Dead Of Night" is an original composition of mine, written several years ago while in a band called Pagan Radio. Recordings of the song can be found floating around the internet on occasion, so keep an ear out.

From film, to literature, to punk and goth-fueled rock and roll, you should now have a pretty good idea of what was pushing the buttons in my brain while working on *The Hurricane Party*.

OF HORNS AND HURRICANES

Readers familiar with my work may be pleased to find the references made to my debut novel *The Horns Of Evangelina*. The connection I have made between the events in that novel and those in The Hurricane Party were part of the intention before I even began working on this book.

It is all part of a larger plan, to loosely tie my individual stories together, to create my own private universe, much in the way that comic book publishers such as Marvel Comics and DC Comics handle their own stories. I even have one of the characters in *The Hurricane Party*, Frankie, be presented as a typical comic book geek (there is a lot of myself in his personality).

The fact that one of *The Hurricane Party* antagonists, Scott, was present during the horrible events of *The Horns Of Evangelina*, is just my first real attempt to bring my stories together. I did this vaguely in my second novel, *The Main Course*, where I briefly mention *Horns* character Collin Monroe's book *The Devil's Lodge*, which gets showcased in *The Hurricane Party* in greater detail.

The Main Course gets a nod in *The Hurricane Party*, mentioning Scott's Hellfire Grub t-shirt. Hellfire Grub is a fictional restaurant mentioned at the end of *The Main Course*.

There are other connections that I wanted to make, but I did not want to overburden the story with unnecessary Easter eggs. The plan is to further bring my fictional universe together in future books.

This is not too different from what other authors such as H.P. Lovecraft, Stephen King and Poppy Z. Brite have done in the past. I plan to explore several genres of storytelling, though always with a dark tone, to create a strange and unique world for my characters to live (and die) in.

I hope that my readers will enjoy this world. Keep reading. It will only get better (and sometimes much, much worse) from here.

THE HURRICANE PARTY TRAILER

Outside, the sky is growing dark with ominous clouds. Inside, a group of friends have gathered together for the weekend.

Outside, the wind begins to howl and the rain begins to fall. Inside, the party has started as drinks are shared and friends reminisce.

"Those pants still smell like fucking Merlot."

Outside, the storm grows worse. Winds tearing trees apart. Rain flooding roads. Inside, the friends listen to the sounds coming from outside.

Outside, three mysterious guests stand at the front door. Seeking shelter. Seeking fun.

"We interrupting a little get-together?"

Seeking to bring inside a storm of hell and misery unmatched by the one on the outside.

"Wanna know a secret? I've got a Little Satan that lives in my belly. He tells me things. He tells me what to do. Do you want to know what he's telling

me right now? I'll give you a hint: You're going to scream."

From **Chuck Morgue**, author of the chilling novels *The Horns Of Evangelina* and *The Main Course*, comes a morose tale of extreme violence, unbridled perversion, and bizarre mystery. A novel so unsettling, the author himself nearly abandoned it out of fear and anxiety. Sure to be one of the most heinous works of literary *"gorenography"* of the decade. An instant splatter punk classic. So close your eyes, hold your breath, and step out into the storm. And then, if you dare, step back inside to..

THE HURRICANE PARTY

You are invited.. To suffer.

HOUSE OF MORGUE

www.houseofmorgue.com
www.myspace.com/houseofmorgue

.KMRG.
99.9FM
THE MIGHTY ROCK GODS!!
COLOR R
RESTRICTED
UNDER 17 REQUIRES ACCOMPANYING PARENT OR ADULT GUARDIAN
COOLHAND MADMAN!
EVENINGS

The Hurricane Party

RSVP ✸✸✸✸✸✸✸✸✸

✸✸✸✸✸✸✸✸ Admit One ✸✸✸✸✸✸✸✸

Look for these other titles available from

HOUSE OF MORGUE

The Horns Of Evangelina
Chuck Morgue, 2007, 160 pages
ISBN 978-0-6151-4363-7

In November 2007, a young man went missing in
the small town of Monterey, Louisiana. The fields
of Evangelina Plantation, where his wrecked vehicle
had been found, were searched for days. Nearly a
week later, the young man's body was found in an
area that had been searched several times. Where
this young man was during his missing week, and
what he may have gone through, is still a haunting
mystery in this middle of nowhere community.
Dark. Erotic. Bloody. THE HORNS OF
EVANGELINA is an exploitation horror novel,
inspired by true events, that will pull you into a
world of psychopaths, paganism, and gut-wrenching
terror.

The Main Course
Chuck Morgue, 2009, 320 Pages
ISBN 978-0-548-01140-0

Donovan Rushing is one of the world's most prolific celebrity chefs. He has seven restaurants and a long-running hit TV cooking show, The Main Course with Donovan Rushing. His epicurean empire is vast and ever-growing, but mysterious forces and secret hands appear to be undermining his power, and his sanity. For this over-worked, over-stressed, schizophrenic alcoholic chef, the line between paranoia and conspiracy are beginning to blur. When a younger rebellious celebrity chef named Eddie Blake appears primed to overthrow Donovan's domain, desperate measures may be in order for Chef Rushing to hold on to his culinary throne. And his mind.

With a plot overflowing with pop culture referencing, and the central characters based on actors Christopher Walken and Johnny Depp, The Main Course is a dark celebrity satire and culinary murder mystery that drags the reader along to a surprisingly violent and bloody climax.

Chuck Morgue is a writer of dark fiction. His work includes *The Horns Of Evangelina* (2007) and *The Main Course* (2009). He lives with his family in a haunted Civil War-era derelict chocolate factory in the marshes of southern Louisiana. In his spare time he hunts dolphins, paints autoerotic landscapes, and unsuccessfully pretends to give a damn about anything other than himself.

www.ingramcontent.com/pod-product-compliance
Lightning Source LLC
Chambersburg PA
CBHW052136170626
46812CB00004B/1458